I0728687

THE WATER FARM

Cecil Bødker

Book Two of *The Water Farm Trilogy*

Translated from Danish by
Michael Goldman

SPUYTEN DUYVIL
New York City

Other translations by Michael Goldman
available from Spuyten Duyvil

Farming Dreams, poems by Knud Sørensen
Stories about Tacit by Cecil Bødker
Fragments of a Mirror, essays by Knud Sønderby
Something to Live up To, poetry by Benny Andersen
Average Neuroses, poetry by Marianne Koluda Hansen

THE DANISH ARTS FOUNDATION

Translation ©2017 Michael Goldman
ISBN 978-1-944682-81-1 pbk.   978-1-944682-82-8 hdc.
Cover photo courtesy of Niels Erik Dreir

Library of Congress Cataloging-in-Publication Data

Names: Bødker, Cecil, author. | Goldman, Michael (Michael Favala) translator.
Title: The water farm / Cecil Bødker ; translated from Danish by Michael Goldman.
Other titles: Vandgēarden. English.
Description: New York City : Spuyten Duyvil, 2017. | Second in a series about
the character, Tavs. Other books, Fortµllinger om Tavs, Malvina.
Identifiers: LCCN 2017032991| ISBN 9781944682811 (pbk.) | ISBN 9781944682828 (hardcover)
Subjects: LCSH: People with social disabilities--Denmark--Fiction. | LCGFT: Psychological fiction
Classification: LCC PT8175.B5465 V3613 2017 | DDC 839.813/74--dc23
LC record available at https://lccn.loc.gov/2017032991

CONTENTS

A Strange Wayfarer

Tacit lowered his hammer, stuck the black piece of iron back down into the coals of the forge, and lifted his arm. Out of habit, his hand grabbed the worn lever handle of the bellows, and began moving it up and down. As if from the breath of a giant, the air pushed out between the coals, and they burst into flame.

A pitiful and sick old giant, thought Tacit, turning so he could look through the door at the gravel, shining yellow in the sunlight. Both doors were opened out towards the road, but it was still dark in the smithy, darker than usual, thought Tacit. Probably because all that sunlight didn't enter the room.

He checked on the piece of iron and then looked out the door again. A long, damp, cold spring was ending. Blessed summer was on its way. The thought comforted him to his bones, and as he stood there, he lost himself in gazing outside, while his arm kept pumping the bellows handle. Pictures from past summers came and went in his inner eye. He stood there, yearning.

At that moment she walked by on the opposite side of the road. She was a slip of a girl, wrapped in clothes like she was expecting a snowstorm, and she was carrying something heavy in her arms. She was facing straight ahead; her gait was that of someone who had been walking for a long time.

Tacit stood there staring, long after she had passed.

He hadn't heard a sound. She hadn't made any other movements except her walking. It was as if she were being led. As if she weren't real. He blinked. Had he fallen asleep? Was he seeing things—here in the middle of the day?

Strange.

He turned back to the forge. The piece of iron had long been white and emitting sparks. And the red light from the coals looked like a hot cave under the broad chimney. He used tongs to lift the iron back to the anvil and started working it with his hammer, though he couldn't shake the sight of her: the way she moved, her gaze constantly far ahead on the road, and her strange clothes.

It was as if she couldn't be bothered to look to the side, he thought. Like someone who wasn't even noticing where she was—just walking. He was sure she wasn't someone from town. There was no one there who looked like that.

So who was she?

And where could she be going?

That road only went to the beach—or to the Water Farm. No one lived out there, far from town.

And her expression, totally closed off, almost glazed over. She looked sort of like someone who was going to go drown herself. That was a discomforting thought.

And what was she wearing? A person didn't usually carry a bundle of things that way—only if it was very heavy or if the person was very tired. Tacit looked over at the blacksmith, standing at the filing bench by the window.

"Did you see her?"

Tacit lowered his hammer, heedless of the iron curling around the horn of the anvil.

"Gypsy," decided the blacksmith without hesitation.

"How do you know?"

"The way she looked –." There was aversion and distance in the blacksmith's voice. "It's best to stay away from Gypsies."

Tacit stood there a while. Then suddenly he laid down his tongs and hammer and loosened his leather apron.

"Are you leaving?" asked the blacksmith brusquely.

"Yeah," said Tacit.

"Is the old lady sick again?"

"No."

"Then what are you doing?"

"What if she's going to the beach? She looked like someone who was going to drown herself."

"What about it?"

With a blackened finger the blacksmith pointed at the piece of iron that was supposed to be made into a gate hinge.

"Take it out of my pay if you want." Tacit hung up his apron on the nail. Then he left.

He turned, not towards town and Granny's house, but out towards the Water Farm, the same way the girl had gone. Her bare feet had left an obvious trail wherever the wind had driven the dust into patches on the road. Strange that a girl like that would just come walking by. What if she went down to the Water Farm and met old Ælgar? There's no telling what would happen then. Ælgar was unpredictable and not friendly to strangers. The thought of their meeting one another troubled Tacit, and he made his way as fast as he could.

She must have been walking rather quickly. He kept looking for the trail in the roadway dust, while his concern turned into worry. Who was she? She didn't look very old.

All at once he realized that her trail had vanished. He had been so preoccupied with his thoughts that he hadn't noticed where her footprints ended. He stopped short and started retracing his steps, looking to both sides. He spotted her, sitting curled up under a big elderberry bush, within the shelter of its branches.

Tacit cut across the roadside ditch to get closer. It was clear she was afraid. She looked up with a frightened expression when he approached, so he stopped with a generous distance between them.

She sat with her bundle on her lap just looking at him.

"I won't hurt you," he said towards her. "You don't have to be afraid."

The girl didn't answer. Her eyes were too big for her slender face.

"I saw you walk by the smithy," he continued, "and I thought you must be lost."

"Why?" she asked dismissively, without averting her stare from him. And suddenly Tacit realized she was sitting there nursing an infant. He looked away, embarrassed, not knowing what else to say. To help reassure her he sat down where he had been standing.

"This road doesn't go anywhere," he answered. "It just goes down to the beach. No one really lives out here. There aren't any real farms this far out."

He thought he noticed her shoulders droop a bit, but she was still on guard.

Then she asked, "What do you mean by that?"

"By what?"

"By 'no one really.'"

Tacit hesitated.

"Who are you looking for?" he asked.

"None of your business."

She's not a Gypsy, he thought, eyeing her hair sticking out from beneath her headscarf. Her complexion was too pale. Her eyes seemed dark; but maybe that was from fear.

He shrugged his shoulders.

"I just thought maybe I could help you," he said.

"Why? You don't know me."

"I saw you go by the smithy. I'm the blacksmith's apprentice—." Tacit realized that he hadn't washed, and that his face and his clothes were black and grimy.

"And so you went out to follow me?" There was disdain in her voice.

"It's just that there's no one here out by the water," Tacit said in his defense.

"Exactly," she snapped. "No one can hear me if I yell." And she casually showed him that she had a knife in her hand.

"It's easy to get lost," he said.

"Thank you. But I can take care of myself."

Tacit's gaze moved to the little round head at her breast.

"Yeah," he replied. "I see."

She flushed with anger, and he regretted it immediately. He wished he'd never said it and tried to smooth it over. Meanwhile, the girl was being fiercely protective of her baby.

"I live with my grandmother," he said.

"Do you think I care where you live?" she snarled. "Don't you think I know what you're after?"

Tacit waited.

Then he said, "I live with my grandmother because my own mother didn't care about me."

The girl didn't answer, but he could see that what he had said reached her. Her eyes opened up a little more—more inquisitive, less dismissive.

"She left me behind when she took off."

"Why?"

"I was in the way. I was a mistake. She abandoned me to go to the city, right after I was born."

The girl just said, "Oh." But her eyes kept looking at him. He thought it was as if she were trying to get a look at him past all the black. What did he look like underneath?

"My name is Tacit," he said.

"Does your grandmother live on this road?" she wanted to know.

Tacit shook his head. "She lives on the other side of town."

"So it's true you were following me."

"I wanted to see where you were going. You looked so tired and no one really lives out here."

"There you said it again. No one really…."

"An old man in an abandoned and dilapidated farm—is that someone?" asked Tacit.

Her eyes peered into him.

"I thought I might go out to the beach," he said, when she didn't answer.

Something inside her relaxed.

"I've never seen a beach," she whispered.

"Where are you from?"

"Inland."

"But where? What's the place called?"

"It doesn't matter."

"I guess not," said Tacit. "What's your name?"

Then again that long searching gaze. How much should she tell? Why didn't he just leave her alone?

After a while, she said, "Malvina."

Tacit looked at her, surprised.

"I've never heard anyone with that name before," he said. "It sounds like the color of a wave out past the breakers."

"My name?" she asked, wondering.

"Yes," he replied. "Blue-green and partly transparent. It's pretty."

"You say strange things," she said.

"What about your last name?" he asked.

"Mandsdatter."

"Mandsdatter?"

She nodded.

What was that supposed to mean, thought Tacit. Wasn't every girl a daughter of a man?

"Yes," she answered.

"You don't say much, do you? Are you scared of being sent back home?" He said it lightly and kind of teasing, but the girl didn't smile. She looked like she was freezing.

He got up.

"I can find a place for you to stay tonight," he said. "And if you dare to, you can walk there with me and I can hold your baby for you."

"There's no need for that," she snapped.

"I'm sure you would get something to eat, too," he said. "When did you eat last?"

"This morning," she said quietly.

"How can you have enough milk for the baby?" he asked.

"There's not enough. I've had to chew up bread for her lately." She took the baby from her breast and put it down in the grass while she straightened her clothes and got up. Tacit saw that she had the knife in her hand the whole time. Not a big knife, but it looked sharp. Short and compact and well-suited for slashing with.

"Is it far?" she asked.

"Not too bad. I can carry the baby—with your permission."

She looked at him, hesitating. Then she nodded and walked out to the road holding the baby. It was already sleeping. She carefully laid the baby in his arms.

"Is it because of her that you left home?" he asked, quietly.

"Why do you ask so many questions all the time?"

"Because it's strange not to know anything."

"It's better that way. I'm leaving early tomorrow morning anyway."

Tacit was just about to ask where she was going, but he bit his tongue and swallowed his question. That would have to wait. She probably didn't even know the answer.

They started walking beside one another down the dusty dirt road.

"Malvina," mumbled Tacit to himself when they had walked a while in silence.

The girl turned her head and looked at him questioningly.

"I didn't know there was a name like that," he said. "It sounds kind of foreign. In my mouth it feels like water from a spring."

"It was my great-grandmother's name."

That shut Tacit up. There was nothing else to talk about. They kept walking.

After a little while he started talking again. "It's not a regular farm," he said.

"What do you mean?" She gave a tired sigh.

"There's no cows," he said.

She looked at him again, questioningly. That sounded strange.

"It's really old," he continued.

"What do you mean?"

"They took the cows with them when they abandoned the place."

"Who?"

"The people who lived there. They pulled them along up and over the hills." Tacit painted a picture for her with his words.

"How can you be so sure if it was so long ago?"

"Granny told me."

"Did she see it?"

"She heard about it from someone who heard it from someone who was there when it happened."

Malvina stared at him, her mouth half-open, still doubting, but riveted.

"Oh," she said quietly.

Tacit continued the story. The words streamed from his lips, conjuring up pictures that first appeared for him back when he was a little tot on Granny's knee. While she knitted, Granny passed on to him what she had heard when she herself was a child.

In Malvina's mind she could see the thaw flooding the farmyard and putting all the buildings' floors under water. And out of the doors, with all their household belongings and linens in big bundles, stepped men and women, holding the hands of their wet, bare-legged children. And all of them started climbing the grassy slopes, followed by their cows, one by one, emerging sopping wet from the barn. The cows were tied together before stiffly making their way out of the water and starting their journey.

He described women and girls who put socks and clogs on the freezing children's feet when they were halfway up the slope. Then they let them go on ahead, while they themselves pulled the reluctant animals to hasten them along. No one knew how long the animals had been forced to stand upright in the flooded barn.

Malvina nodded. She wasn't paying attention to where she was going anymore. Tacit thought she probably wasn't used to hearing someone tell her stories. She probably never sat against someone's knee while the continual clicking of knitting needles blended with crackling from the stove as it died out; and it was all bound together with stories about regular people and supernatural creatures, events both good and bad, some true, some fabricated.

When he stopped talking, Malvina asked, "Where were they going?"

"No one knows," said Tacit. "They left and never came back. The story belongs to the farm that had to stay behind, down in its hollow."

"What about the water?"

"It's gone now. For a very long time the farm was deserted. No one dared to settle in a place like that. Until one day a man came by and stayed there. He slept in the farmhand's room so no one would mind. He was going to leave the next day.

"But the Water Farm wouldn't let him go. It needed someone to be there, and he decided to stay one more night. The next day he looked in all the rooms and saw how desolate they were, how grass and thistles were growing through the old walls, how the floors were rotting and decomposing at the edges. He tried to imagine the people who had lived there before, what they might have been like.

"And he went out and looked in the empty, abandoned barns, and felt the quiet that lay all across the bottom of the hollow and blanketed the farm. And he walked in silence, keeping the old farm company, while it slowly died. He wasn't a regular farmer. He stayed there with his horse."

"A horse?"

"Right."

"Was he a kind of hobo?"

"Yeah, I guess."

"Can a person beg if he has a horse?"

"I don't think he ever begged."

"Did he work?"

Tacit shook his head.

"What did he live off of?"

Tacit turned his head and looked at her coyly.

"He got by," he told her.

This affected Malvina. Her expression closed off and she looked away.

"He took only what he needed to survive," Tacit said. She probably doesn't take well to being teased, he thought. But the subject interested her. A hobo.

"He never talks about it," continued Tacit.

"What does he live off of now?" she asked.

"Boiled fish," laughed Tacit. "And boiled mussels and boiled potatoes. Sometimes a bit of cabbage; and in the winter—cooked field beets."

He could tell that she was really trying to figure out how this all made sense.

"Fish?" she said. "What do you mean 'fish'? Pickled herring?" She didn't believe him. "That costs a lot of money."

She's from inland, remembered Tacit. There, fish are always salted and pickled and cost money.

"He catches them himself," he answered.

Her eyes got wide. Dumbfounded.

"You're lying," she said uncertainly.

"There's a beach." Tacit realized she was rather naive.

"Can you do that? Can you catch them yourself?"

"Sure," answered Tacit, not offering to show her the beach. Not yet.

When they got to where they could see the roofs below them, Tacit stopped. From three sides the grass sloped steeply down towards the farm. Towards the back there were woods that started just behind the barn and continued through the ravine all the way out to the ocean. The girl beside him lost herself in the view, and Tacit looked directly at her face without feeling awkward. He saw her eyes move from building to building and down from the farmyard up over the grass and back again—measuring, searching.

He knew it was because of the cows. She knew about cows; they were part of wherever she had come from. Finally she woke from her reverie with a little twitch.

"It sure is strange," she said, turning towards him with her thoughts full of what he had told her about the Water Farm. Her eyes rested on the child, asleep in his arms.

"Yeah," he said.

He started walking down the wheel track that had become just a narrow path from disuse. She followed him reticently. In front of the buildings she stopped. Just in front of the first gable there was a place where the earth had been worked. It was the only sign that anyone lived there.

"That's for potatoes," Tacit told her. "I dug that bed."

"Didn't you say that someone lived here?" Suddenly she was on guard.

"Someone does."

"Then why did you dig the bed?"

"Because he's old and has a bad knee."

She stood and listened.

"Why is it so quiet here?"

"No one makes noise here."

She looked at him suspiciously.

"You're lying. There's no one living here. Don't you think I know why you led me down here. Give me my baby."

"Just a second. After you see I'm not lying."

"Give me my baby." She lifted the hand with the knife.

"Stay right here and you'll see." Tacit paid no attention to her demand and ignored the knife. He stepped out into the middle of the farmyard and let out a high, thin whistle. Then he stood there, waiting.

Suddenly around the corner of the house, a child came running out with her arms lifted, heading right at Tacit.

Malvina stood there, thunderstruck, staring. If the child had instead risen from the cobblestones next to Tacit, she couldn't have been more astonished.

It looked like a girl on account of the long curls, but the clothes were more like a boy's—earth-tones and coarse. Holding the baby in his one arm, Tacit bent down and caught the running child with his other arm, and Malvina saw how the curls bent over the bundle, apparently without the child's knowing what it was.

Tacit walked towards her carrying both of them.

"This is Mina," he said, giving the girl a little hug as she hid her face in his neck at the sight of the stranger.

Malvina stood there, letting her surprise subside. So it was a girl.

"Is she yours?" she blurted out.

Tacit shook his head.

"Not the way you think. Her mother abandoned her here. She's three." He handed the infant back to Malvina and placed Mina down next to himself. She hid behind his pant leg while keeping an eye on the stranger.

"I want to stay here," said Mina, clinging to his leg. "I don't want to go."

"You're not going anywhere," Tacit comforted her, crouching down next to her and putting his arms around her. "You don't have to be afraid. This isn't your mother."

"It's not?" The girl looked up surprised at the stranger. "Why isn't she?"

"This is a different lady."

The word tugged at Malvina, who took exception to being called a lady. But her protest didn't find a way of being expressed. The whole conversation seemed peculiar.

"Why?" asked the child again, as if the only possibility were that this woman was her mother.

"She's just going to sleep here tonight," answered Tacit.

"Here?" The child turned her head and looked at the dilapidated house. "Why?"

"Because she doesn't have anyplace to go."

"Why doesn't she?"

"Because she's out walking with her little baby."

"But I'm not going with her," answered Mina, pulling herself close in to Tacit.

"Not you. Her own little baby," he said.

"Where is it?" Mina looked past Malvina to see if someone was hiding behind her heavy skirts.

"She's never seen another child," explained Tacit, glancing up towards Malvina. "Granny has tried to tell her about it, but she's never met any. Would you show her your little one?"

Malvina didn't move, as if she didn't hear what was asked. Her expression looked completely confused. Then she knelt down suddenly and opened the bundle.

The infant awoke and whimpered. Mina stepped back, afraid. There was something moving in there.

"What is it?" she asked, terrified, holding onto Tacit.

"It's a baby," said Malvina.

"From a pig?" she asked. "It doesn't look like the one we had."

"It's a people baby," continued Tacit patiently. "Once you were little like that."

Mina shook her head vigorously.

"All people start out being very small," said Tacit.

"It's a pig," maintained Mina. "It's just wrapped up."

"It's a little girl," said Malvina.

The three-year-old looked at her doubtfully.

"How do you know?" she asked.

Malvina carefully began to unwrap her baby from the various rags and pieces of clothing swaddled around her. Unceremoniously she removed the bit of moss from up between the baby's legs and tossed it aside.

"It got dirty," Mina said without hesitation.

Malvina smiled. She started to grasp the situation.

"Have you ever seen a pig?" she asked. "A real pig?"

Mina pulled back farther and nodded.

Then Malvina asked, "Have you ever seen a pig with hands and fingers like this?" She spread apart the baby's fingers and showed them to her.

Mina shook her head, perplexed.

"Or feet like this?" Malvina lifted one of the baby's legs so it came free from the swaddling cloths.

Mina just looked at her.

"Who has hands and feet like that?" asked Malvina.

Mina looked quickly at her own hands and then hid them behind her back.

"Do you still think she looks like a piglet?" Malvina raised up the baby, put her in a sitting position and held her that way. "With hair like this on its head?" She lifted up some of the baby's thin, blonde hair.

Mina unconsciously put her hand up to her own hair, and Tacit hid his smile.

Around the corner of the house appeared an old man. He was wearing a heavy coat and had an axe hanging from his one hand. He approached them with suspicion, staring continuously at Malvina.

She quickly bundled the pieces of clothing around the baby and picked her up while she herself rose to her feet.

"Who is that?" asked the man with the axe, stopping just short of them.

"I'm not completely sure, yet," answered Tacit.

"What is she doing here?"

The old man's gaze moved to the three-year-old who, detecting the old man's mistrust, clung again tightly to Tacit.

"Her name's Malvina," said Tacit gently. "She's from inland someplace. I said she could sleep here tonight."

The old man grunted dismissively. Then he turned abruptly and walked away mumbling. Around the corner of the house he disappeared, followed by Malvina's alarmed stare.

"He's not as bad as he seems," said Tacit.

Malvina regained her composure and turned towards Tacit with a shudder. "I can't stay here," she whispered.

"He thought you were someone coming to take Mina away," Tacit said.

"Take her away—?"

"Her mother. Or someone from the parish. He's really afraid someone's going to find out that she's here."

"But that axe—"

"That wasn't meant for you. Come with me."

He started walking across the farmyard, and Malvina followed him reluctantly, ready to flee at any moment. They passed through a half-open plank door that bridged the gap between the farmhouse and the old barn. In the angle between the two buildings there was a kind of small courtyard. Against the barn gable lay a large pile of chopped branches, and next to them, a stout chopping block. The old man was standing with his back to them, and he didn't turn around when they passed by. His axe chopped the branches into short pieces with a steady rhythm.

Then Malvina stopped with a gasp. Tacit heard her and

turned around. As if paralyzed, the strange girl stood staring at the thick, rusty iron pipe sticking up out of the ground at the far end of the little courtyard. The clear half-circle of water around the pipe held her fast. The little pool received the water after it splashed down into the long stone trough. The water kept coming and coming.

"It's still here… the water—" she whispered.

"It's always been here," he answered just as softly.

Then he led her to the back door through the scullery and into the kitchen, where he showed her the bed.

"You can sleep here," he said.

Malvina protested. "I can sleep in some hay in an outbuilding," she said.

"But here's a bed."

"But doesn't someone sleep in it?" she asked.

"Not any more. Mina's mother used it before she left. That was three years ago. When she was gone, Ælgar took the baby with him over to the farmhand's room. He never wanted to stay in here."

"What about you?"

"I stay at Granny's," said Tacit.

"So there's no one else here except those two?" Malvina looked around at the dilapidated kitchen.

"Just the horse and a couple of chickens."

"It sure is strange."

"It's a good place if you want to be left alone," said Tacit.

"Is that what he wants?" She motioned with her head back towards the door where they came in.

"He's scared that someone will take Mina away from him if people find out she's here."

"Why would someone do that?"

"People think he's a murderer."

"A murderer?" Malvina stood up with a start from the edge of the bed. "How can he be taking care of a little child?"

"There you see, you're no better than everyone else who judges him without knowing anything." Tacit's voice was bitter.

"Isn't it true?"

"He served a sentence for a murder he didn't commit. He took the blame to cover for someone else."

Malvina sank down on the edge of the bed again. Her eyes hung on Tacit.

"She got married to a third man while he was doing time," he said bleakly.

Malvina looked down at the floor. "Sorry. That was a dumb thing to say."

"I didn't say that to make you feel bad," said Tacit. "It's just that people are so quick to judge."

She nodded. "I know. It's happened to me, too. That's why I had to leave."

Tacit waited. But she didn't say anything else.

So he said, "It must be hard to walk carrying a baby in your arms."

She nodded slightly.

"I'm dead," she replied.

"Dead?"

It gave Tacit a start. She looked like she meant it in all seriousness. But he didn't dare to ask, didn't want to press her.

"I'll tell the old man to give you something to eat tonight," he said instead, and turned towards the door.

Malvina sat there as if she hadn't heard him. Her eyes were distant.

Then Tacit left.

SALTWATER COD

The following day Tacit hurried to the Water Farm right after work—maybe she would still be there.

He didn't really think so. She seemed like the kind of person who didn't stay anywhere very long. She seemed hounded, and Ælgar's discontent certainly wouldn't help.

On the other hand, he hadn't noticed her pass by the smithy. All day long he had been conscious of positioning himself to keep an eye on the road outside. And his thoughts kept returning to how she said she was dead.

Dead how? What did she mean?

He turned it over again in his mind. Was she condemned in some way? Could it be she had some terminal illness? He winced at the thought. Or had she done something she could be sent to jail for? Is that what she meant by dead—that she had no future?

Though it was fruitless, his thoughts continued probing the few things Malvina had said about herself. He would have liked to have known more.

The layers of clothing she wore couldn't hide the fact that she was very young and unbelievably thin. How could she even have the strength to carry around a baby that was no longer a tiny newborn? What was compelling her?

It was completely quiet when he walked down the grassy slope, and the farmyard was deserted as usual. He let out his normal whistle, but little Mina didn't come running. She must be with Ælgar on one of his excursions, he thought. The old man always took her if he had something to do. She sat in front on the horse, and if he furtively borrowed a boat on the beach to do some fishing, he tied a rope around her waist and attached it to the thwart—or to a tree if he went to the marl pit. Tacit figured that the girl stranger was gone as well.

Nonetheless he walked around the gable to the kitchen door. The water from within the earth's crust stood there gurgling just as it had the day before. The iron pipe poured out its liquid, undisturbed, to the edge of the trough, and the axe was planted firmly in the big chopping block.

But the door to the scullery wasn't closed, and he heard voices.

He could hear it was Malvina and little Mina, and he pushed the door open carefully to look inside. In the middle of the kitchen floor, Mina was taking a bath in the old scullery tub, and sitting upright on the bed, Malvina was nursing her baby. She was telling Mina a story.

Suddenly Malvina lifted her head, saw Tacit there, and blushed.

Tacit walked over to them.

Both Malvina and Mina observed him with startled expressions, as if they had been caught red-handed in something they weren't allowed to do.

"I hope it's alright that I gave her a bath," apologized Malvina. "It's just that the water was there already. I gave the little one a bath, and then Mina wanted one too."

Tacit said it was perfectly fine, and hid his relief that she was still there by bending over and feeling the water in the tub.

"Is it nice?" he asked.

Mina giggled and put both her arms underwater.

"I'm washing myself," she said proudly. She fished up a scrap of torn cloth from the bottom and pushed it around her face with both hands.

"You are getting so big," said Tacit. "Where's Grandpa?"

"He rode down to the beach."

"To fish?"

"I don't know."

"I'd better go down there and see how he's doing." Tacit

straightened up to go.

"You have to dry me first," demanded the girl in the bathtub, rising quickly so water flowed over onto the floor.

"Look out," said Tacit, stepping aside.

"I always do that when Grandpa gives me a bath," said the child.

"I'm sure you do," said Tacit, looking around for something to dry her with. "It's just that I don't like to get water in my clogs." He reached for a piece of cloth he noticed hanging on the stove handle.

"No, that one's wet," said Malvina, feeling behind her in the bed where she found a towel. "Here—."

Tacit wrapped the towel around Mina and lifted her out onto the floor. Then he rubbed her dry.

"There you go," said Tacit, turning again to leave.

"My clothes, too," demanded Mina. "I want clothes on, too."

"Don't you think I should go down and help Grandpa now?" asked Tacit.

Mina thought about it.

Then she said, "Me first."

"Come up here in the bed," said Malvina, "and I'll show you how to do it. Then you'll be all ready when they come back."

The child looked back and forth between the two. Then she climbed up in the bed where her clothes were lying.

"You are getting so spoiled," teased Tacit, laughing.

Malvina gave him a quick look but didn't say anything.

When he got to the door he turned around.

"Do you think you could keep the fire going in the stove?" he asked carefully, meeting Malvina's gaze. "And heat some water in the pot? Just in case the old man catches something."

"Sure," she answered without hesitation.

Servant girl, thought Tacit. The way she helps in the house— her acquiescence. It was different when she was sitting under the elderberry bush ready to defend herself with a knife.

He checked himself. He knew so little about her, and he was glad that she hadn't left.

Tacit made it to the beach just as Ælgar was pulling the borrowed boat back to its spot. He used the horse. It had stood tied to a tree while he was out, but now he had stuck the anchor under the front thwart and wrapped the rope around the horse's chest while he walked and held the railing.

Stretched out on the bottom planks lay two very large codfish getting sloshed in seawater with the boat's jerking movements. For some reason, Ælgar was bothered that Tacit had come. Ælgar didn't look at Tacit and he tried to keep his back to him.

"Big fish," said Tacit, looking past the old man down into the pram. "It looks like you've been out by the buoy today."

Ælgar mumbled something dismissive without denying it.

When Tacit didn't say anything else, Ælgar said in his defense, "You've got to have decent food sometimes." But that left a suppressed insult hanging in the air. It was dangerous to go fishing alone out by the buoy.

"Really?" asked Tacit, "Isn't it usually good enough, the food you get?"

Ælgar answered bitingly, "Did you really think that I was going to put out the usual miserable freshwater cod for her, the new one?"

"What's wrong with them?"

"Small fry," sneered Ælgar.

"Are you trying to make an impression on her as a big-time fisherman?" Tacit poked at him. "So she'll really feel like it's a great place to eat? —So she'll stay? That's it, isn't it?"

Ælgar leered at him and growled.

"You don't even know what she's like," Tacit said. "Or what she's done."

"No different than the rest of us," grumbled Ælgar. "Had a baby—at the wrong time—with the wrong person."

"We? You mean Gunhilda?"

"Yeah. And myself."

"You?"

Tacit looked at him, wondering. The old man was really worked up. Agitated. This was the second time a woman had come to the Water Farm with a little baby—and this time it had to go better. This time she had to stay—he needed that.

"Yes, me," snapped Ælgar. "You know I had a baby out of wedlock, and with the wrong person."

"And haven't I paid a price for it?" he said. "And what about you? Where did you come from? Your mother—."

Tacit stood silently. It was rare that old Ælgar revealed anything from his past, but he clung onto it, there was no doubt of that. It still ate at him. Tacit had thought that all that from the past had receded into the background since he had taken in Mina, with all the happiness and all the worry and anxiety that came along with it.

But it was also clear to Tacit that it would be less risky to have Mina at the Water Farm if there were also a grown woman there. There would be less chance that someone from the parish came and took her away. That must be what was on the old man's mind.

"She says she's dead," said Tacit.

"Who's dead?" Ælgar spun around on his stiff leg and glared at him viciously.

"Malvina. She said that yesterday."

"Well, as long as you're not dead. She just needs a place to stay. —And she is just about dying from malnutrition."

"But that's what she said. I'm sure there's a lot we don't know. Something is plaguing her."

"If you're thinking she's going to leave, you had better keep your distance for a while." Ælgar's tone was short and cold while he stuck a finger behind the gills of the fish one at a time, fastening a string through them. "If you're hanging around, waiting for her to leave, she won't feel welcome. People pick up on that kind of negative thinking, in case you didn't know."

Tacit cowered a little.

Ælgar sounded threatening. He walked over and slung the cod over the horse. Then they all walked together back through the woods in silence. Ingelin followed on Ælgar's heels. He and Tacit thought about the strange girl with the baby. Why had she come? And what could they do to make her stay?

It was hot in the kitchen when they arrived. There was a fire in the wood stove and a pot quietly simmering on top. Both Ælgar and Tacit sniffed the air.

"I asked Mina if you ate potatoes sometimes," said Malvina quickly and dismissively when she saw them.

"There aren't any potatoes," hissed Ælgar as if it had been an insult. Something he ought to have provided.

"But I found a field beet."

"That was for the horse," said Ælgar.

"That's what Mina said too, but I took it anyway. The horse can have the peelings." She handed the cracked clay dish with the peelings towards Ælgar with both hands.

I guess she's more than just a simple maid, thought Tacit.

Then Malvina caught sight of the codfish hanging from Ælgar near the ground. They startled her, and she walked backwards, terrified, towards the bed.

"What is that?" she asked.

"Ocean fish," blurted out Ælgar in a tone both proud and threatening.

"They don't look at all like the herring we got inland," she answered.

"It's not herring. It's cod," Ælgar told her.

"And you're not inland anymore," said Tacit.

"But can you eat them?" Malvina looked at the gaping fish heads dubiously. She still had the dish in her hands.

"I'm going out to clean them," said Tacit, taking the fish from Ælgar and carrying them outside to the spring. There he rinsed them and cut them into pieces. He gave the guts to the chickens who came running immediately. Ælgar walked behind him with the clay dish.

"Huh. Peelings," sneered Ælgar, shambling by on his stiff leg.

Tacit cut the heads off the codfish without responding. Then he took the fish into the kitchen and cut them into smaller pieces.

"That sure is a lot," exclaimed Malvina. "How is all that going to fit in the pot?"

"We can cook two rounds if we have to," said Tacit. "If there's some for tomorrow, all the better."

"Yes, tomorrow – " Malvina stopped and looked up at him.

"Ælgar will be upset if you don't appreciate his catch," said Tacit. "He was all the way out in the ocean current to get some really good food, because you're here. It would be an insult to leave without eating it. You know it's not easy for an old man to row all the way out there, and it's not without danger either."

"I don't want to be any trouble." Her voice sounded uncertain.

"He will be really upset, terribly disappointed, if you leave tomorrow."

"Why are you doing all this for me?"

Tacit noticed something behind the question. But he wasn't sure what it was.

"Don't you like being here?" he asked, to bring it to the surface.

Malvina looked to the side.

"Of course," she nodded. "It's not that."

"Then what is it?"

"I just can't stay here."

"Is that something you've decided?"

"Yes."

"Is it because you're dead?"

She tossed a sharp glance his way. "Yes," she said bitterly.

"That's why."

It was quiet for a little while. Tacit didn't want to press her. He had to try a new tack.

"What if there was some purpose for your finding your way here?" he asked quietly.

Malvina's eyes slid to the side where, on the bed next to the sleeping infant, Mina sat, trying to understand what they were talking about. Tacit followed her gaze.

"She needs you," he said. "The old man won't live forever."

"Don't try and force me," she mumbled in warning. "The last place I stayed the woman wanted to keep me there too. She wanted me to work for the farmers in the village while she took care of my baby."

"I'm not trying to force you," said Tacit.

"Then what are you trying to do?"

"You need a place to stay."

"It's not my fault if the parish comes and takes Mina away." Malvina's voice was sharp and despairing.

"No," answered Tacit. "But it is your fault if your own child loses her mother."

Her eyes opened wide with horror.

"You are suffering from malnutrition," he said. "There are limits to how much hardship a person can take."

"It's not my fault –" she started to say. "You could take care of her."

She looked at him without seeing; she looked right through him, and he was startled by what he witnessed. She filled up with something that made the blood vanish from her lips and her knuckles protruded while she stood there in the middle of the floor with her fists clenched. She had difficulty breathing. It was like she was swaying—her eyes wide open the whole time.

Tacit reached out and grabbed her just as she fell. When Ælgar came in a few moments later, she was lying pale and motionless on the bed.

"What happened?" asked the old man, staring at Tacit in disbelief. "What did you do to her?"

"Nothing. She fainted."

"A person can't run around on the road in that condition." Ælgar was agitated.

"In what condition?"

"Can't you see that she's no more than skin and bones? And with a nursing baby!"

"Then why don't you give her some goats milk?" growled Tacit.

"There's no more milk in that goat. You know that."

"Then fatten it up."

"You can't do that from one day to the next," said Ælgar combatively. His voice shook a bit, and Tacit realized that Ælgar had been out and had tried.

"I can get some from Granny," suggested Tacit, trying to smooth things over.

"The devil you can. You'd better keep your mouth shut about her being here. We don't want anyone snooping."

"It's only Granny. She doesn't gossip." Tacit sounded a bit offended.

"Raw cod liver," Ælgar shot back.

"What?" asked Tacit confused.

"She needs raw cod liver."

"You're crazy," said Tacit. "No one eats that."

"I do," proclaimed Ælgar, tossing his head.

"Me too," uttered Mina from the bed where she was curled up in a corner.

Malvina made a movement and they saw that she was awake. Her eyes appeared conscious.

"What happened?" she asked weakly.

"You fainted," said Tacit.

Malvina tried to get up.

"No, stay lying down," he said quickly. "I'll cook the codfish."

"Raw cod liver?" she mumbled.

Tacit tried to comfort her, lowering his voice. "You don't have to listen to what he says."

"What is it good for?" she asked.

"All kinds of things," answered Ælgar convincingly. "Just look at Mina." He pronounced it 'Meen.'

"She's healthy," he said proudly.

Malvina shifted her gaze to the little girl at the foot of the bed. He was right, she seemed healthy and strong with clear eyes. Malvina observed her for a while. It was also obvious that her skin was clear. Then she turned back towards the old man.

"I'll try some of that," she said firmly.

Ælgar straightened up, his shoulders broadened in his old heavy frock coat. He turned towards the kitchen table under the window, took out the bread on the shelf below, and the knife on the windowsill, where Mina couldn't reach. Solemnly he cut four robust slices and replaced the knife. Then he went out and came back with his hands full of dripping wet raw cod liver.

Tacit was startled.

"Where did you get that?" he asked.

"From the chickens, of course. You're so grandiose you just throw it out on the ground. Then I have to chase away the chickens to get it."

"But I had no idea—." Tacit glanced at Malvina, then looked away again.

He sensed that she was laughing an invisible, silent laughter.

"No, you didn't know. You don't know anything," hissed Ælgar angrily, while his hands spread a thick layer of cod liver on three of the bread slices. Then he sprinkled a bit of damp, gray salt on top.

He took out the three mismatched plates, one of which hadn't been used since Gunhilda left, plus Mina's little tin bowl. Then they ate the white codfish in big flakes with beet pieces, and a bit of the cooking broth to dip into. The three of them had their cod liver sandwiches as well, while Tacit ate his bread dry. Malvina ate hers sitting on the bed. Something was still churning inside her where no one could see. Simmering. Tacit could sense it without even looking at her.

Little Nameless, Comfort Child

"What's your baby's name?" asked Tacit on the third day. They were sitting on the stoop outside near the spring.

"She doesn't have one. She wasn't baptized."

"But what do you call her?"

"Nothing."

She sounded dismissive, like she was hiding something.

"Not even a nickname, like just between you two? Mina had lots of names before we found the right one for her." Tacit made it sound completely natural, even though it wasn't entirely true.

Malvina glanced at him a bit shyly from the side.

"I call her Comfort," she said softly.

"Comfort?"

"Yes, or Comfort Child, or Little Nameless—and a bunch of other things. But not a name."

"Isn't Comfort a name?"

"No."

"Why do you call her that?"

"For a long time she's all I've had. She's all I've had to comfort me, since the berry harvest."

"She can't be that old," said Tacit. "Not unless she's very small for her age."

"She was born three weeks after mid-winter," answered Malvina sharply.

"Why the berry harvest then?"

Malvina lifted the baby from her lap and cuddled her. "That was when I was pregnant," she said. And Tacit could sense how she retreated into herself.

"There's a lot I don't know," he said, sighing.

"It might be better that way," said Malvina.

They sat for a while, watching Mina play with the twigs by

the chopping block.

Then Tacit revived the conversation. "Was it there with the woman you mentioned?"

"What?"

"That she was born."

"No."

"Wasn't she nice? The one that wanted you to stay?"

"Sure. She brought me into her bed the night I came there."

"Then why didn't you stay?"

"It wasn't far enough away."

"From what?" Tacit pursued her steadily down what he thought was a trail.

"From everything." Malvina squirmed on the step. She said under her breath, "I shouldn't have told you about her."

"I'd like to hear more about that woman."

"It's not worth it. You don't know her anyway."

"Are you far enough away now?"

"I can see it would be convenient for you if I stayed here," she answered darkly.

"And for you too," responded Tacit.

"What do you mean?"

"A place to be. A bed to sleep in. Something to eat. Warmth. A good place for your child. No one will bother you here."

Malvina just looked at him. Doubtfully. Searchingly.

"Tell me about Gunhilda," she asked then, abruptly.

Caught off guard, Tacit lifted his head without answering. He would need a little time before knowing what to say. What parts should he tell?

"Why did she leave?" asked Malvina before he had a chance to begin. "If this is such a great place as you say, why didn't she stay?"

"It was different with her," said Tacit slowly. "She was older than you, and she was used to a different kind of life." He groped for the words to describe what had happened with

Gunhilda back then.

"Wasn't she happy here with all of you?" asked Malvina bluntly.

"It wasn't enough for her just to be safe. She wanted a more active life—a life in a city. And she didn't care about her baby. Meen was like a ball and chain to her," he said. "That was why she left the girl here." Tacit quietly shook his head.

"Meen," repeated Malvina gently, like Ælgar.

"Gunhilda would never have dreamed of choosing a life wandering the roads with her child," Tacit said. "She was raised with other expectations. Meen stayed behind when she disappeared."

"Did Gunhilda name her?"

Tacit shook his head.

"Gunhilda gave her nothing but the minimum. It was Ælgar who talked to the baby and played with her. And it was Ælgar who named her after Granny, because she helped Mina come into the world. Granny's name is Pedermina."

"Meen," said Malvina again, smiling weakly. "He is fond of her."

"It would kill him if someone came and took her away," mumbled Tacit. "He has cared for her all this time."

Malvina sat, lost in thought, and Tacit let her sit undisturbed for a long while.

Then he asked, "Where is Ælgar now?"

"I don't know. He didn't say. He just rode off."

"But he left Mina here with you?"

"Is that so strange?" Malvina looked at him questioningly.

"Actually, yes," he answered.

"He did it yesterday too," she said.

"Can't you see it? Can't you tell what's happening?" Tacit sounded surprised.

"But I'm used to taking care of children," said Malvina. "I have always watched my younger brothers and sisters. Why shouldn't I be able to watch Mina?"

"That's not what I mean," said Tacit. "It's that he lets you. He has never let anyone watch her before. He usually takes her with him wherever he goes. Ever since Gunhilda left, he has kept her with him day and night."

Tacit gave her a penetrating look.

"Don't you understand?" he said. "You have only been here a couple of days and already he trusts Mina in your care."

"Well I don't really know him—not really," admitted Malvina hesitantly.

"No, but he trusts you that much," said Tacit.

Malvina blushed and looked down.

They sat in silence again, watching Mina play.

Then Tacit asked, "So how did you come to have a baby?" He thought it was about time for her to tell a little bit more about herself.

But Malvina turned suddenly towards him. Her body was tense and her expression closed and impenetrable.

"What business is that of yours?" she sputtered angrily. "Why do you even ask? Why do you keep pestering me? You go on acting all friendly, but you just want to pry into my business. Just stop already! The baby is mine alone, and no one needs to know where it came from—not you or anyone else."

It was a powerful outburst. She was panting, and Tacit realized he had touched a nerve.

Trying to keep his voice placid, he asked her, "If you're so certain about that, then why are you hiding?"

"You asked me that yesterday. Why do you have to keep prying?"

"To get you to talk."

"Why should I tell you anything?" Malvina's voice was shaking.

"Because I want to know who you are."

"What does it matter? I'm not going to stay here anyway."

Her words hit him like a sucker-punch. But he forced himself to go on.

"Why won't you stay here?"

"Because I won't."

"And why won't you?"

"Because you keep pestering me."

It felt like hitting a brick wall, and Tacit sat there silently for a long while, feeling hurt. He remembered back when Ælgar had tried to drown himself and his horse, how the old man had berated him for pulling him out, and how he had to battle with Ælgar for weeks because he couldn't bear to see the old man die.

Why couldn't he just leave things alone? Including Malvina. Just let her go her own way if she absolutely wanted to, taking with her her baby and her anguish. Why did he have to get all mixed up in it?

He sat silently for so long that he almost forgot about the girl sitting next to him. So long that she realized he was upset.

Quietly, she said, "Tell me some more about Gunhilda."

Was she reconsidering? Tacit regained his composure. Was there a crack in her facade? A crack named Gunhilda?

"Why?" he asked without looking at her.

"Because I'd like to know who she was."

It was almost a repetition of his words, and Tacit felt a glad warmth inside. It was as if she had reached out her hand.

He began softly, "Ælgar found her out by the roadside, lying in the ditch, having contractions."

"Oh," uttered Malvina.

"The man she was married to had thrown her out. Someone had told him the child wasn't his."

"And he believed it?'"

"He pushed her out the door and locked it. She had to leave."

"Was it true, then?"

"If it weren't she probably wouldn't have left—she could

have gone to her parents."

Malvina thought quietly without answering. And Tacit wondered to himself if she were comparing her own situation to Gunhilda's. He didn't interrupt her.

She sighed. "It can happen a lot of ways," she mumbled, almost inaudibly.

Tacit nodded and waited.

"And what else?" she said abruptly.

"He set her on the horse the best he could, took her home, and put her in his bed in the farmhand's quarters."

"Ælgar?" A wave of disgust crossed Malvina's face.

Tacit saw it.

"It was the only bed on the farm," he said quickly. "He let Gunhilda have it, and he slept in the moldy hay in the attic."

"Oh," said Malvina. She sounded apologetic.

But she had revealed something without naming it, thought Tacit. Her discomfort was just as much for herself as it was for Gunhilda.

"And then Granny came?"

"Yes, we got her as fast as we could," he said, omitting to tell her how he had lit the stove to heat up water, which started a chimney fire, and they had to stay up all night brushing water on the rafters and the roof.

"And then Mina was born here?"

"That's right."

Malvina looked straight ahead with a serious expression.

Very quietly she said, "At least she had a woman to help her."

Tacit was puzzled. What did she mean by that? He was just about to ask if she had given birth in secret, or something like that, but he swallowed his question. Another time, he thought. He had to show restraint.

"And then she left?"

"No," he answered. "She stayed here through the winter first. But it was obvious this was no place for her. She didn't like it here. She left after Mina was weaned.”

“That she could do such a thing,” mumbled the girl on the stoop.

“She’s not the first one to do something like that,” said Tacit with an emphasis that made her think about his situation.

“I was only a few weeks old when my mother left,” he said.

She shook her head.

“I don’t understand how someone could do that,” she said.

“I know. Comfort is very lucky,” said Tacit.

“You think there’s something lucky about being born out of wedlock?”

“Sure I do, with that father.”

Malvina was shocked.

“What father?” she asked, tossing her head. Anger and fear wrestled in her expression. “What do you know about him?”

“Nothing,” admitted Tacit. “Only that he didn’t want anything to do with the baby—otherwise you wouldn’t be sitting here.”

Malvina’s shoulders sank.

“He doesn’t even know,” she whispered.

“You haven’t revealed it?”

Malvina hesitated. Then she shook her head.

“He must be one of the finer people.”

Malvina could no longer control her expression.

“Won’t you leave me alone,” she pleaded.

He stopped talking.

After a little while he said, “Comfort is a very lucky baby—with that mother.”

Then there was only the sound of the spring water splashing into the trough. Tacit was afraid Malvina was going to cry. What would he do then? What were you supposed to do when a girl started crying? He decided to change the subject.

After giving it some thought, he said, “There’s some clothes.”

“Clothes?” Malvina didn’t know what he was referring to.

"From when Mina was little," said Tacit. "Granny brought them. Gunhilda didn't have anything. You can have them."

Malvina winced.

"I guess you noticed that she's bundled in rags."

"It's hard not to notice," answered Tacit. "But it's nothing to be ashamed of. You might as well use Mina's old clothes. They're on the shelf over the bed."

"Thank you," whispered Malvina.

Tacit wasn't sure if she would follow through with it, maybe because it would make it look like she was going to stay. She hadn't given any real sign of that yet. It was obvious she didn't want to be tied down.

Just wait and see, he thought. That's the way she was.

Muffled hoofbeats told of the arrival of the horse in the farmyard on its unshod hooves. Tacit rose immediately and walked out through the gate, and Mina dropped what she had in her hands and darted past him. In wonder, Malvina watched her go. There was no doubt that the little girl adored that old man with the stiff leg.

Out in the yard, Ælgar loosened a torn potato sack, letting it slip down onto the cobblestones, while Tacit walked over and clapped Ingelin on the neck. He carefully ignored giving any attention to the sack or asking about it. But he quietly followed the old man, as he led the horse with one hand and held Mina with the other, to the little courtyard with the water trough, where he let the horse drink.

"It's impossible to find potatoes this time of year," mumbled Ælgar apologetically. "All the furrows are empty."

"Yeah," answered Tacit, to show he was listening. There was nothing that could rile up Ælgar more, than if he weren't paying attention.

"They've harvested all of them." continued Ælgar.

"They're probably starting to sprout now, too," said Tacit.

Malvina was gone from the stoop. She had retreated inside

with her baby. Mina had the old man's full attention. She begged him for a ride, and Ælgar lifted her up on the horse and let her ride across the farmyard to the grassy slope, where he lifted her down again and let the horse go.

"But I got some really nice field beets," said the old man with satisfaction. "They emptied a beet pile and forgot so many under the straw that it filled up the sack. So now we have them."

"I wonder if maybe I should make the potato bed a little bigger this year," mumbled Tacit pensively to himself.

Ælgar gave him a quick discerning look. Had she said something? Did the lad know something that he hadn't heard himself? He had trouble thinking of Tacit as anything other than an overgrown boy.

"No, you shouldn't," growled Ælgar.

"But what if she stays?"

"Did she say that?" The old man scrutinized him.

"It's good to be ahead of things," said Tacit.

Ælgar fumed. "The devil it is. That's the kind of thing that made Gunhilda leave. I told her about everything I had planned to make it better for her to stay here—about the garden beds, about more chickens, whatever—and about the goat. It was the goat that made her leave."

"How was that?"

"Have you forgotten that she was weaning Mina and then one day she just disappeared? What more do you need to know?"

"She would have left anyway," said Tacit. "It wasn't because of the garden beds or the goat. It was just as much for her own sake that she weaned Mina."

Ælgar scowled. "Why?"

"Then she wouldn't have to go into town with her boobs full of milk." It made Tacit cringe to say it out loud.

"Don't you dare start digging in the potato bed now," said Ælgar.

"You could use some more potatoes yourself, if it comes to

that," defended Tacit. "You never have enough with what is there now."

"Just let it be."

"Wouldn't it be nice if we had some potatoes for her right now?" Tacit said, knowing that he was touching on a sore point.

"If field beets aren't good enough for you, then why don't you go home and eat with Granny?" Ælgar said.

"And seed potatoes?" continued Tacit. "Where will you get them? Who is it every year who gets you some to put in the ground?"

It was a continual affront to the old man that every year Tacit brought a sack of seed potatoes, which he had earned by doing some side work for a farmer.

"I don't want you to start digging anything," Ælgar said. "She hasn't decided, and you don't touch that piece of ground."

"She's not like Gunhilda," answered Tacit combatively. "Malvina will take Comfort with her if she leaves."

Their voices were belligerent and little Mina looked back and forth from one to the other, alarmed. Then suddenly she turned and ran away, crying.

The two men stared at one another accusatorially.

"There you see," said the old man. "You upset her."

"It was you," answered the young man. "You always have to be so damned stubborn."

Inside the kitchen, Malvina looked up concerned when the crying child came storming in.

"What's wrong, little one? Did you hurt yourself?" She opened her arms wide and embraced Mina. "What's wrong?"

"They're arguing," stammered the child.

"Who's arguing?" Malvina held her close.

"Tacit and Grandpa."

"What are they arguing about?"

"About you."

"About me? It'll be alright, you'll see." Malvina took a rag and dried the snot and tears from Mina's face.

"They say you're going to leave, that you won't stay here." And a new wave of crying erupted from the child.

Malvina rocked her back and forth. "There, there. I'm sure they didn't mean it like that. They'll make up again."

"But is it true? Are you leaving?"

Malvina dried the child's messy face again before she answered.

"I'm not sure yet," she said.

"But you have to stay," pleaded Mina, pushing herself away so she could look up. And Malvina stared searchingly into the child's wide teary eyes.

"What if I stay just for a little while?" she said hesitantly.

It was obvious that Mina didn't know what a little while might mean. But she heard a concession.

After a pause Mina asked, "For always?"

"I can't say," said Malvina.

"Then how long?"

"What if I stay for the summer?"

"Is that a long time?"

"I think so," said Malvina.

"Is that the same as forever?" A glint of confidence emanated from Mina.

A soft rustling made them both turn towards the door where Tacit and Ælgar stood together, staring at them. How long had they been there? Had they heard what was said? Was she trapped? Thoughts swirled in her head. Then her anger took over.

"What are you two staring at?" she yelled. "I can leave right now if you're going to be like that. —It is so cowardly of you to use the girl to manipulate me." Malvina let go of Mina and stood up.

"We didn't use her," protested Tacit.

"Then why does she come in here howling that I have to stay here forever?"

"But we didn't use her," he said again.

"I will not be forced into anything. I've been forced into enough things. I'll leave right now –."

Malvina's face went white and her voice trailed off and this time Tacit didn't reach her in time before she fell to the floor.

Tacit pushed Mina over to Ælgar and picked up Malvina. She was so light. So easy to lift. He laid her carefully on the bed next to the infant and turned around. Mina stood against Ælgar with her hands over her ears and her eyes open wide as if in shock.

"Don't be afraid," he told her. "It wasn't your fault. Malvina is feeling sick. We have to take care of her and give her something to eat so she'll feel better."

Mina just looked at him. Ælgar had already snuck out through the scullery.

"Come here and we'll make some food," suggested Tacit, to help Mina be herself again. "Run out to Grandpa and get a really nice beet; the best one he has."

The girl livened up and hurried out. Carefully, Tacit pulled a blanket over Malvina; then he walked out to the spring. He picked up the tin pail with the lid that was floating around in the trough. Inside was the leftover fish from the day before.

A little while later Mina came in proudly with a huge shiny beet held tight to her chest.

"Here," she said. "Grandpa scraped off the dirt."

"Great," answered Tacit, taking the ladle. "Now lay it on this dish so you can wash it."

Tacit set the clay dish down on a chair and poured in some water. Then he lit the oven and put the pot on. As soon as Mina was finished with the beet he started cutting it into pieces.

The Eel Cake

The next time Tacit went to the Water Farm he brought Granny. The old woman sat straddling the horse he led, and she did not look enthusiastic about being transported in this way. Her skirts were bunched up around her on the horse's back, and her thin legs, in black woolen socks which she wore all year round, stuck out below. She was not pleased that the multiple darnings were visible.

She had protested when he said that he wanted her to come. Her knees were hurting; she couldn't walk that far. And besides, she didn't see why it was necessary.

"You're needed," he had answered.

"Is someone sick?" She thought of Mina and was immediately more sympathetic.

"I'm not sure what you call it. There's a girl there; she's very thin and she keeps falling down. Ælgar says it's malnutrition."

"A girl?" Granny wrinkled her brow. "What kind of girl?"

"If I go and borrow Niels Peter's horse, can you sit on that, and then I'll tell you on the way?"

Granny hesitated.

"You have to come," insisted Tacit. "There's an infant, too."

Granny was reluctant.

"How long have they been out there?" she asked.

Tacit told her.

"And you are only first telling me now?" Granny sounded offended. "Go and get the horse," she ordered.

Tacit disappeared. Meanwhile she collected what baby clothes she had from when Mina was little, and tied them in a bundle.

"Do you have a few potatoes you could spare?" he asked when he got back.

"You can take what's there; we'll find some more," she responded.

It was Tacit who insisted she straddle the horse, and not sit side-saddle like she wanted to.

"You have to sit securely," he said, "so you don't slide off."

Granny sighed and did as he asked. She held the bundle in front of her, and behind her Tacit fastened the half-sack of potatoes that was in the house. He figured that would give her something to lean against.

Then they left.

"So tell me what you've gotten yourself mixed up in."

Tacit walked next to the horse with one hand on the halter while he told her about the day he saw the strange girl walk past the smithy. He thought it odd that it had only been a week ago.

Granny listened silently. As soon as he had mentioned there was an infant, she had been wondering if he were the cause of it. But that wasn't the case, according to what he said. Several times she asked him to repeat word for word how the strange girl had responded to one thing or another. Tacit could tell that Granny didn't want to arrive unprepared.

Tacit helped her dismount at the edge of the farmyard. Then he loosened the sack of potatoes and walked over to tie off the horse at the bottom of the grassy slope. Ingelin was nowhere to be seen, so Tacit figured Ælgar must be on one of his excursions. And he wondered if perhaps Ælgar was purposefully leaving Mina alone with Malvina as much as possible, so they would bond with one another. That had to be what he was trying to do. Otherwise he was never away from the farm as much as he had been since Malvina arrived.

When Tacit turned back towards the farmyard, Granny had already shaken her skirts into place and disappeared; only the potatoes lay there. So he grabbed hold of the sack and carried it into the scullery, where he set it down in a dark corner, so it wouldn't be the first thing Ælgar saw when he came back.

When Malvina heard the horse's hoofbeats in the farmyard, she thought it was the old man arriving, but when there was a knock on the door and a strange woman walked towards her into the kitchen, she was terrified. With all the talk she had heard about someone coming to take Mina away, she thought the moment had come. She thought someone had heard about the child and sent a woman to explore the rumor. And here she stood all alone. What was she going to say?

Malvina's terror was sensed immediately by Mina, who didn't understand what was wrong, but knew that it was something bad by the way Malvina tried to hide the child behind her.

The old woman greeted Malvina and looked slowly around the kitchen, which seemed somewhat changed since her last visit.

Malvina didn't answer. Her heart was beating through her chest.

"Where is Granny's little Mina?" asked the old woman.

"Here!" shouted the girl, darting across the floor to Granny, nearly knocking her over.

Granny. Of course. The relief was so tremendous that Malvina had to sit on the bed. Pedermina looked her up and down.

"So you're the newcomer?" she asked.

Malvina put her hands up to her cheeks. "You really scared me," she said.

"What are you afraid of?" Granny asked.

Malvina looked at her, confused. Did Granny know something?

"Did you do something wrong?" Granny asked again.

"It was mostly on Mina's behalf," she said.

"But also partly your own?" The old woman's eyes rested scrutinizingly on her. "You seem quite young to me to have a baby."

"I turned fifteen," responded Malvina.

"Not long ago," said Granny.

Malvina looked away. "In February," she said.

Granny sighed. "Poor girl. Do you have any milk for the little one?"

"Not much."

"That's what I figured. You look pretty spindly. But Tacit says you won't talk about what happened to you." Granny looked at her questioningly, but Malvina just weakly shook her head.

"Okay. Can I see your baby?" Granny entered the room and Malvina turned on the edge of the bed and picked up the infant.

"It's a girl," she said.

The baby opened it's sleepy eyes, and Granny slid her hand up into the swaddling clothes and felt the baby's legs.

"She's in better shape than you are, but she doesn't have any extra," Granny said. "What are you feeding her?"

"The same things I eat. I chew them for her."

"It sounds like you've had younger siblings," Granny said softly. "You chewed their food for them while your mother was working?"

Malvina nodded bashfully.

Granny felt bad for her. Even though she didn't know the cause of the girl's misfortune, she understood enough to know that it wasn't the girl's intention to end up like this.

"I brought some clothes for the little one," said Granny, looking for the bundle that she had laid down.

"They let me use clothes from this shelf here," answered Malvina meekly. She felt like the old woman could see right through her, and already knew what had happened.

"It's good to have enough," said Granny, spreading out the baby clothes on the old quilt, covering the bed. Watching her, Malvina felt her own heart soften.

"So did you give birth in secret?" asked the old woman, looking askance at the girl.

Malvina shuddered. She knew that was against the law.

"No," she whispered. "Not that."

"Then what? You didn't give birth with your mother," Granny said.

"How would you know?" Malvina tried to offer some resistance.

"Well," answered Pedermina, "no mother sends a newborn baby out on the road, even if it is her daughter's and even if the baby is unwanted."

They looked at one another.

"Someone helped me," Malvina whispered.

"Who did?" asked Granny, skeptical.

"I can't tell you."

"You can tell me. What are you afraid of?"

"It's not something you can tell. It's too strange."

Granny observed her thoughtfully. Then she asked, "Was it a person?"

Malvina nodded. "Yes, it was a person."

"Then it was the baby's father?"

"No!" The answer was like a scream. Then Malvina composed herself. "He didn't know about it," she said, almost inaudibly.

"So you haven't made it known?" asked Granny, just like Tacit had done.

"No—yes—I don't know—." Malvina was at a loss as to how to explain.

Outside, Tacit was pacing around, not knowing how to occupy himself. He wanted to ask Malvina where Ælgar had gone, but when he stepped into the scullery, he could hear by Granny's tone of voice that she was doing something that should not be interrupted. He was sure of that. He couldn't first, almost forcibly, make her come along to the Water Farm to save the situation, and then afterwards get in her way. He would have to wait.

But he could start digging the potato bed a little larger, since he was here anyway. Resolutely he went into Ælgar's room and took a hayfork. The old man was always very particular with his tools and washed the dirt off of them after each use and put them away in his room. They were all made of cast-off things that he had found, and made useful again with new handles that he had carved—from an old board or a broken wagon hitch or whatever he could find. Sometimes he went into the woods and brought back an ash branch to carve to fit.

Tacit plunged the fork into the earth and started digging, but he didn't think he had gotten very far before Ælgar rode into the farmyard, at a walk, from the opposite side. Ælgar stopped short when he saw the strange horse grazing there peacefully. Then he turned his gaze to Tacit who continued working the garden bed, sifting out large clumps of quack-grass roots, tossing them to the side while Ingelin came closer.

"What happened?" asked Ælgar tensely. His voice was flat and ready for anything.

"Nothing," answered Tacit, straightening up. "Granny is in there. She wanted to take a look at Malvina."

"And the horse?"

"It's one I borrowed. Her knees were hurting too much for her to walk that far."

"And Meen?"

"She's in there too."

Reassured, Ælgar glided down from the horse. A sack hung over his shoulder on a rope, and there was a bulge in it.

"What's in the sack?" asked Tacit, curious.

The old man cackled triumphantly.

"Something new," he said.

"It's moving," said Tacit, staring at the sack.

"Eels," said Ælgar.

"Eels? But didn't they wreck your trap—that must be a few years ago now. Wasn't there someone who took it up and cut it to pieces?"

"Yeah." A dark cloud drifted across the old man's face. "I knew what they meant when they said I had placed it in the eel run. I didn't try and repair it. And I stopped trying to catch eel."

"Well then what are you doing now? How did you catch those—there's more than one, isn't there?" Tacit felt the outside of the sack.

"Two," said Ælgar.

"Did you use an eel spear?"

The old man shook his head.

"I never liked eel spears. They're too unreliable and too many eels get damaged."

"Well, what then?"

"A trap, of course."

"But—." Tacit looked at him.

Ælgar gave a serious laugh. "I know what you're thinking," he said. "But you should know that I have never stolen anything from another man's trap."

Tacit hesitated long enough that Ælgar knew he had guessed right.

"Then where did you get an eel trap?" asked Tacit, immediately realizing that that question wasn't much better.

"I made it myself, of course. What else?"

"You found some chicken wire?"

"There are lots of willows growing down by the peat pits," the old man said.

"Willows? Can you make eel traps out of willows?" Tacit didn't believe him.

"They did in the old days," said Ælgar. "My grandfather did. He made willow eel traps for other people. My father had some, but he didn't use them because they rotted too fast."

"And so you just went and made one?" Tacit laughed, impressed.

"Well, not just like that, but I figured it out. I never really knew how to make them, I just knew how they looked. I've been making traps all winter."

"You have?" Tacit was surprised.

"You didn't know that." Ælgar cackled with satisfaction. "You don't know everything, do you?"

"I guess not," said Tacit.

"They didn't work anyway. They didn't catch anything."

Tacit stayed quiet.

"But today there were some in it. The one I have now works." Ælgar sounded victorious and he loosened the top of the sack so Tacit could look in. They were nice eels.

"So where did you put it?" Tacit wanted to know.

"In one of the ditches by the peat pits. No one will look for traps there. How about we go inside?"

"Inside?" Tacit looked doubtful.

"I want to show them to Granny," responded the old man with thinly-veiled pride.

Tacit stuck the fork in the ground and followed him. Ælgar hadn't made a stir about his digging, despite the warning the old man had given him. It must be the eels.

It was quiet in the kitchen. Malvina sat on the bed, nursing her baby. She looked like she had been crying. And Granny's mouth was tense. She was rummaging at the stove, making a racket.

Tacit wondered if maybe they had come in too soon. Had the two women finished what needed saying?

Ælgar looked from the one woman to the other. Had something changed? Granny had made some dough, which lay rising on the clay dish, and now she was cleaning the oven with a stiff brush. Little Mina sat right up against Malvina, as if the child had been trying to comfort her. The mood was different, but there was no sign of anyone leaving. So he took a step forward.

"Eels," he exclaimed, patting the sack, which set the catch to squirming.

"Eels?"

Everyone's attention was suddenly on the old man. Eel was not everyday food. It was for celebrations and special occasions, and they each went and looked in the bag. Conversation sprang up again and became almost jovial.

"Me too," pleaded Mina, wanting to be lifted up. Tacit swept her up and leaned her forward to look down into the sack, where something was moving.

"What is that?" she asked with big round eyes.

"Eels. You heard him."

"But what are eels?"

"A kind of fish. A very delicious fish," said Tacit. "It's the kind you eat when it's a special day."

"Is it a special day today?" she asked, looking around.

It was quiet. Who could answer that?

"It is," responded Granny. "It is a special day today. Even if it is a regular Sunday."

The others looked questioningly at Granny. But she didn't elaborate.

"If it's alright with Ælgar, we can make an eel cake out of this dough here," she said instead.

The old man straightened up, surprised.

"I haven't had eel cake since I was a little boy. I didn't think it existed anymore," he said, his expression softening.

"I've never heard of such a thing," said Tacit skeptically. He turned towards Malvina. "Have you?"

She lifted her head, but retreated quickly back into herself again. Then she nodded.

"But I've never tasted it," she said. "Only the farm owner was allowed to catch eels." She glanced shyly at Granny, and Tacit got the sense of a kind of connection between the two women, some confidence they shared. Had Granny gotten Malvina to come out with who she was and where she had come from? He thought so.

"Are you going to kill them yourself?" asked Granny, looking at the sack.

Ælgar straightened himself up. What did she think?

"I have some kindling," continued Granny, now looking at Tacit. "But I don't have any wood."

Tacit took the old peat bucket and walked out to the shed. Ælgar was right behind him, and he walked over to the shed too, and grabbed a sturdy piece of firewood. Tacit watched him go out the door and over to the water trough where Ælgar emptied the eels out onto the grass.

It gave Tacit a start. Now the eels are going to run in opposite directions and get away, he thought. But the old man was just as quick as the eels, and he struck them each a blow to the head with the firewood. That slowed them down quite a bit.

Tacit filled the basket with wood and carried it inside. As he passed the water trough, he saw Ælgar grab the closest eel while taking his folding knife out of his coat pocket. He made a deep cut, half-severing off the head, splitting the eel lengthwise, and removing the innards for the chickens. Then he loosened the skin on top and peeled it off while holding the head. Just as Tacit reached the scullery door, a cleaned and skinned eel plopped down into the water trough.

When Tacit came out again a short while later, the other eel was also cleaned and lying in the water, while the two chickens fought over the organs. Tacit refilled the basket with firewood and carried it back inside.

It was warm now in the kitchen, uncomfortably so. Tacit inspected the stove. He was glad that the old man had installed the fire bricks that he himself had brought over. He could still see the memory of the chimney fire burning clearly in his soul. And Granny liked a hot stove.

When the dough had risen she dumped it out onto the countertop and kneaded it thoroughly. Then she cleaned the dish, and since there was no fat, let alone butter, in the house, she took the largest and fattiest of the eels and rubbed it against the dish.

Then she placed some dough on the bottom, cut up the eels and laid several pieces on top. Then she laid more dough and more pieces of eel on top, until both eels were gone and the dish was full to the rim.

Everyone sat quietly watching Granny's hands. Once in a while it seemed like Pedermina wanted to be sure that Malvina was paying full attention.

"It's good that you're paying attention," said Granny. "Next time you'll be doing this."

What did she mean by that? Tacit was sure there was some secret meaning behind her statement. Also in the way Malvina retreated into herself when everyone suddenly looked at her. There was something the two women knew that the rest of them didn't quite know yet.

Granny went and opened the oven door with the tip of her clog, then stuck her hand halfway inside to check.

"Now it's getting somewhere," she said to no one in particular. Then her eyes met Malvina's, who immediately got up and went over and put her hand in the oven next to Granny's.

"Now it's almost ready," said the old woman.

Then she straightened up.

"I have hired Malvina," she said clearly, looking around. If she had pulled a burning piece of wood from the stove and thrown it at their feet, it couldn't have had a bigger impact. Both Ælgar and Tacit were startled.

After an appropriate pause Granny continued. "She is employed for the summer. She will live here and take care of little Mina and keep house for Ælgar. For that she will get meals for herself and her baby and some clothing—whatever I can get my hands on."

The old woman's eyes wandered from person to person. "In the fall, we'll see," she added soberly.

It was quiet for quite a while.

Then Ælgar shook himself loose from the table and walked over towards Malvina. She looked at him surprised.

"Welcome," he said, holding out his hand as if she had just walked in the door.

"Thank you," whispered Malvina, taking his coarse hand and curtseying. Granny's mouth seemed satisfied; now things were as they should be.

"The oven!" she exclaimed as she swung around so her skirts spun out from her legs.

Malvina bent down quickly and opened the oven door while holding the edge of her dress so she wouldn't burn herself.

"Feel it," said Pedermina. And Malvina held her hand at the oven door opening.

"It's hotter now," she said. "Much hotter."

"That's that way it should be." Granny picked up the dish with both hands and pushed it into the heat.

"Don't you have clogs?" she asked, looking at the girl's bare feet.

"They're too small," Malvina answered softly. "But I don't usually wear them in the summer."

"No, I guess you don't." Granny's voice was knowing and matter-of-fact.

Ælgar and Tacit went outside. The eel cake was going to take a while to bake. They would have to wait. Ælgar went to his room and got another pitchfork.

"If you do the digging, "said Ælgar, "I'll break up the earth and take out the roots."

They walked over to the potato bed and, in his quiet mind, Tacit blessed the old woman who was his grandmother. Ælgar seemed more agreeable than he had ever been, and for once they worked without bickering. Tacit couldn't remember when it had ever been like this—maybe back when Gunhilda was there.

"Eel cake," mumbled the old man to himself, following behind Tacit's digging. "I'm really going to have eel cake."

Tacit kept digging and didn't bother Ælgar. It was faster this way, more than twice as fast as if he had done it by himself. And Ælgar didn't say 'stop, that's enough.' They worked continuously until, a couple of hours later, Malvina came out and told them to come in and eat.

The old man stuck his fork in the ground.

So that's not even enough. Tacit planted his own tool where he had stopped. Back when Gunhilda was there, Ælgar had fantasized about a garden—a real vegetable garden—with many kinds of vegetables, not just a potato bed. It never amounted to anything. He insisted it was those plans that made Gunhilda leave.

But Malvina was employed. Granny had gotten her to stay by simply hiring her outright. She wouldn't leave even if Ælgar manifested his old dream. Not now.

Inside on the table stood the eel cake in the baking dish. High and golden brown it jutted over the edge of the dish, and the smell was different than regular bread. It was inviting, thought Tacit, more celebratory.

Ælgar too stopped inside the door. Just stood there. His face was raised, his head projected forward. His nostrils twitched.

"Oh," he sighed, breathing in the kitchen aroma. "That I should live to see this day."

Then Granny, with a long, worn-down bread knife, loosened the eel cake from the dish and slid it out onto a short, broad wooden plank they used as a cutting board. It was a piece of wood Ælgar had found on the beach that was white—bleached and washed by the seawater. He couldn't bring himself to burn it, so he used it as a wooden plate instead. That was before he had found the other dishes—one in the ground where there had once been a chicken yard, and two others in a low spot which had been used to dump extra dirt.

Ælgar looked around. They would have to make room for a lot of people at the table. There were two chairs that he had once cobbled together, and there was the short bench that was there when he had first arrived. He hesitated. Should he get the little chopping block from the scullery for himself? At one time it probably had been used for slaughtering chickens and geese.

"You sit here," said Granny, interrupting his thoughts before he had reached a conclusion. She pointed to the chair closest to him. "I'll take this one, then the two youngsters can share the bench. They don't take up that much room."

Ælgar sat down without resisting, and picked up Mina on his lap. She stared at the eel cake. Tacit figured that she had never seen any kind of cake in her life.

Standing, Granny slid the knife through the crust and down through the soft interior, where the baked eels' skeletons gave some resistance before yielding, and where the loose crumbling dough blended with the eel drippings. It was tantalizing. A real celebration. No other farm-maid's hiring party had ever been sealed in such a manner on this farm. Ælgar inhaled the aroma reverently and deeply. Nothing must go to waste. The world, life, and everything had just now reached its joyful culmination.

Steam rose from the eel cake's interior. Broad and grand, it stood on its salt-scoured board, filling the room with well-being. The sight of it symbolized the realization that Malvina would be staying there at least for the summer, and the knowledge that Ælgar had caught eel in his own trap, that the trap worked, and that he could catch more. He felt the festivity pulsing in his veins with no misgivings. This time he trusted the woman, young as she was, because when Granny had made a pact with her, it would stick. A whole summer. He didn't dare think farther ahead than that. What would come afterwards he couldn't say. He wouldn't occupy himself with that just yet.

On the other side of the table, with her back to the window, sat Malvina, rosy-cheeked, next to Tacit. Despite the heat of the room she felt a sense of relief and well-being. Since she had let herself be hired by the old woman, and not by Tacit or Ælgar, she felt freer. They couldn't make demands of her, and she could stay without being beholden to either of them. She hadn't promised them anything and they had no power over her. Not that she felt afraid of either of them, but they were both men, even though the one was rather old and the other one quite young. Here she had no master and that meant a lot to her.

And she wasn't going to live on charity. She had to earn her room and board, for her baby as well, and perhaps some clothing. Now that she had a place, she felt freer and she could allow herself to be more approachable. It felt safe.

Granny knew what she was doing. Her questioning had gotten the girl to tell at least some of how she had gotten into trouble. Granny had no doubt there was more to it, seeing how the girl was scared to death and had cloaked herself in secrecy, because it was the only defense she had against what she had been through. But she had told Granny enough that the old woman knew generally what had happened and could act accordingly. Granny could tell by the mood in the room that she had made the right decision.

Everyone followed the path of the knife through the eel cake with great concentration while she cut good-sized pieces for each person. Ælgar got the first piece. No one moved before everyone had a piece in front of them, and Granny had said *Enjoy the meal* and sat down. And most of the eel cake was still left uncut.

It tasted just as it should. Ælgar's head nodded up and down while he chewed and his fingers grew shiny from holding his piece of eel cake. He had never tasted anything so good, he mumbled, sucking carefully on a stump of eel backbone, before laying it on the table. And on his lap, Mina chewed away vigorously. Granny had removed the bones from her piece before giving it to her.

Of all the times Granny had been brought to the Water Farm through the years, none of the visits had been as peaceful as this one. She felt satisfied. Besides, there was something about the strange girl that appealed to her, without her being able to put a finger on what it was. A poor man's daughter—that was obvious. No farmer would allow a daughter of his to travel the roads. If she got into trouble he would bring her back home and lock her up—or drive her to some relatives far away where she wouldn't cast shame on her immediate family. Malvina's barefootedness was genuine, she was sure of that,—but her name? What day-laborer would dare call their daughter Malvina? That could easily be judged as haughtiness.

On the other hand, if the girl decided to change her name to that herself, then her upbringing wasn't as impoverished in mind and spirit as one might have expected.

When no one could eat another bite, there was still some eel cake left. One after another they got up and went out to drink from the ladle at the water bucket. "Spring water," said Granny, drying her chin.

"Water from inside the earth," said Tacit. "The best water in the entire parish."

"The most dangerous, too," added the old woman.

Then she took her shawl and laid it across her shoulders as a sign of leaving. She was ready to go home now, and Tacit didn't protest. The party was over.

But not for Ælgar. His eyes had changed, and Tacit looked at him, wondering. The old man's eyes were blue. Tacit had never noticed that before, had never thought of it. Ælgar's eyes always tended to hide so deeply under his perturbed brow, that Tacit never noticed the color. But now, for once, Ælgar had had some luck.

Silver

"Is he sick out there or something?" asked Granny's neighbor, when Tacit asked to borrow his horse for the fourth Sunday in a row.

"Not actually sick," said Tacit, "but you know how it is when you get older—with arthritis and things like that."

"Can your grandmother help him with that?"

"I don't think anyone can, not really. But just that she comes by—I can repay you by shoeing the horse next time it needs it," answered Tacit, pointing to the mare that stood there sniffing him curiously.

"Oh, it's not that—." Now it was Granny's neighbor, Niels Peter's turn to be evasive. But Tacit knew that he really wanted to have the horse re-shod.

He led the horse to Granny's house. She always had various odds and ends to bring along. There was always something going on between her and Malvina that he didn't involve himself with. A person didn't need to know every little thing. But still he thought that the old woman's bundles were getting bigger all the time.

And Granny didn't tell him anything. She had never been very talkative, and when something was occupying her, she got even more silent. It wasn't until the horse came tramping into the farmyard and little Mina came dashing over in a bright summer dress, that something started to dawn on him. Granny laughed when she saw Mina and the ecstatic child laughed back.

"You look so nice," said the old woman, as Tacit lifted her down from the horse.

"Malvina sewed it."

"She's getting really good, isn't she?"

Mina jumped up and down in place, not knowing how to answer. Then she was handed the smallest bundle and marched off carrying it next to Granny, who bore the rest, past the farmhouse, around to the back door. Tacit pulled the horse up the slope and moved the tethering pole. Remnants of conversation from the previous Sundays appeared in his memory and began to form a pattern.

One time Pedermina asked, "Haven't you ever learned how to knit?"

"Not really," said Malvina. "I always had to darn socks. I darned all our socks in the winter, and I had to collect the yarn myself by picking tufts of wool off of bushes and fences and make it into yarn on the spindle." Tacit noticed a hint of pride in her story. This was a task she had mastered. But Granny just sighed.

"Dear God, child. How are you going to survive in this world if you can't sew or knit? And with a little baby?" The old woman shook her head.

"I would like to learn how," whispered Malvina.

Granny looked lost in her own thoughts. But now Tacit realized that Granny was deeply involved with teaching Malvina the necessary skills, and whether the girl stayed at the Water Farm or not, it would be invaluable knowledge for her.

And not just that. Once Granny got started, she would probably show Malvina lots of other things too. He thought about all the shirts and socks that she had knitted from scrap yarn when he was little. How she took a bowl of water and sat herself down with it when she had unraveled something; how she dipped her fingers repeatedly in the water while she pulled the curly yarn taut and shiny into big skeins. And how she lay the damp coils to dry on the stove shelf before she started knitting something new from the old yarn.

The kitchen was already strewn with pieces of cloth when Tacit came in. Mina was standing in her bare feet on top of the unsteady table that Ælgar and Gunhilda had nailed together from random pieces of wood. It wobbled every time the child moved.

Tacit stood there, but no one had time to notice him. Something had to be fixed on the fine new dress, and Mina had to stand patiently with her arms out. Tacit was going to ask about Ælgar's whereabouts since Ælgar normally would be gone by this time of the morning.

Tacit knew that he had made a crow trap, a twig cage in which he used fish scraps as bait, with a door that smacked closed when a crow hopped into it. Ælgar had been proud as a peacock when he showed it to Tacit, but Tacit hadn't heard anything about if it worked, or if the crows were too smart for it.

Spurred by a sudden idea, Tacit left the kitchen and walked into the next room where he hadn't been in years. There wasn't any reason to go in there; everything looked pretty much like it had when he was there before. The floor was perhaps a bit more moldy and gnawed by mice and age. It must have been the farmer's sitting room; the windows faced the farmyard. He stood there for a while looking around, thinking about the first time he walked through it. It had been with the girl Camilla. She was scared to be in there.

One day he would take Malvina and show her around all the rooms in the house. She wouldn't be afraid; he was sure of that. He walked deeper into the house to the great room, which was as wide as the house and had windows out to both the farmyard and the garden. In this room would have stood their finest furniture, chests with church clothes and extra blankets, chests with things used by the woman of the house like tablecloths, bedsheets and things like that. And perhaps some silverware, spoons and forks that only appeared at weddings, baptisms and funerals.

Tacit walked along the walls, looking at what was left of the old wallpaper. There were several layers, but the patterns and colors were no longer apparent. Most of it was chewed off the walls, which gave the room a blotchy and neglected impression. The floor was dilapidated as well. In many places it had sunk down and lay directly on the earth below. All along the garden side he could see the foundation stones, because the boards no longer reached all the way, and grass and weeds poked through the wall. All the boards felt spongy and Tacit walked with care.

He still stuck his foot through when he went to look more carefully at the old wood stove that stood in the middle of the partition wall with its back to the foyer and the proper entrance. A cloud of fine brown rotted wood-dust rose up from the hole and a chunk of the mite-infested board came up when he lifted his foot back. That's too bad, he thought. He didn't mean to destroy anything or disturb the peace in the room.

Through the hole, he could see the edge of the large ashlar stones that formed the base beneath the wood stove. It looked like the earth had been disturbed there, as if something had dug underneath the masonry. Maybe an animal was living there. Maybe rats?

He stuck his foot back in the hole and poked in the dust with his toe, and something shiny appeared. He bent down and picked it up. A coin?

He looked at it closely, and rubbed it firmly with his fingers. No, it wasn't a real coin. Most of it was worn down so the pattern on it wasn't recognizable. It wasn't anything. He was going to toss it into the hole again when he saw there was one more.

Strange. It didn't look like any kind of money he'd ever seen. He knelt down and felt in the hole under the ashlar stones.

At first he thought he had grabbed a dead animal—a dried-out rat or something like that. It was skin in any case. But when he pulled it out it was not rat-like, even though it was hide with a bit of fur on it.

He reached in again and grabbed a handful of earth mixed

with coins. Tacit stared at them. What were they? And why were they stuck underneath the base of the wood stove? Many of them were completely black.

He spit on one of them and rubbed it hard with his thumb. It wasn't rusty iron, like he thought. It got shinier. Could it possibly be silver? He sat a long time staring at what he had in his hand.

If it were silver, why didn't they take it with them when the water came, when they took everything else they had? Why would they leave the money behind? And why didn't they come and get it when they realized they had forgotten it? Or didn't they even know it was there?

Tacit's mind swirled while he attempted to imagine that people had been living for generations at the Water Farm without knowing there was a cache of silver underneath the wood stove. That someone long before had hidden it there.

A silver treasure? What should he do?

He started sweating underneath his shirt, and then he got a chill and a shiver ran through him. His hands were shaking as he spread the earth across the floorboards and picked out the coins. There were more underneath, and he dug feverishly. One turned up, then four, then nothing, then one, then a couple more. Some of them were tiny, and some of them were big and heavy, but none of them looked like modern money. He kept digging until a long time had passed without finding any more. Then he collected together what he had and put them in his pocket. Not just one pocket, he had to split them up so they weren't so obvious. Then, with his foot, he scraped the dirt back into the hole and walked back to the kitchen.

"What are you up to?" asked Granny suspiciously.

"I'm waiting for Ælgar," he answered.

"Inside the house?"

"I haven't been in there for a long time. The floors and the ceiling are very rotten," he said, before continuing to walk out through the scullery and over to the old barn to find a place where he could get a good look at what he found, without being interrupted.

He wandered around the old outbuildings for a while without finding a place where he could be totally safe.

Safe from what?

He wasn't even sure himself. Everything seemed confusing. What if? Or what if? The coins in his pockets were cool on his thighs, and he needed a place to collect his thoughts.

Why hadn't he shown the coins to Granny?

Or to Malvina?

He felt like a thief. What had he done?

At last he crept up to the loft over the cow stalls and cautiously found a place where a bit of light fell through a hole in the thatched roof. There he sat down and brushed away dust and old hay from a section of the clay surface that covered the floor. There he emptied out the coins.

It was the Water Farm's money. It had to be. From olden times it had lain there while the people on the farm changed and the water chased away the last ones. It had lain there while Ælgar lived there and while the farm decayed all alone.

Enough money to repair it.

But maybe the money wasn't usable anymore. Could money get to be too old?

He sat for a little while sorting the coins by size. There were so many. He tried to read what was on them, but he couldn't tell. Some of them were so worn that half of the letters were missing, and where there were letters, he couldn't tell what they meant. But he could read the years. On one of the big ones it said 1564.

You can't buy anything with money like this, he thought.

He sat some more.

Then what should he do with them?

He didn't know.

What would happen if he showed them to Ælgar?

Tacit was at a loss. He had never seen so much money at one time, and he couldn't answer any of the questions swirling in his mind. There must be enough here to buy a whole house—a whole farm, maybe. If they were worth something.

What if he showed them to Granny? What would she say? That it was the farm's money? That he should let them be? That it would bring bad luck if he took them?

But he had already taken them.

He sat looking at the coins, fingering them. Where should he put them? He couldn't keep walking around with them in his pockets. They were too awkward and heavy. But where was it safe to store them?

He could bury them someplace until he figured out what to do. But then he would have to have something like a bag or a jar or something like that. The old skin they had been in wasn't usable anymore. It was too rotted.

But where could he find something like that on this desolate abandoned farm, where everything they found they were using. And Ælgar knew exactly what was left in all the outbuildings, and he would demand an explanation if something went missing. And he couldn't go take something from home either. Granny would also want an explanation.

But the rest of the farmhouse? Could there be other things that they didn't take with them when the water rose, things Ælgar didn't know about, since he always kept a distance from the farmhouse. Tacit was sure that Ælgar had never been anywhere else but the scullery, the kitchen and up in the attic. He'd never seen the rooms. He probably had never even looked in the windows.

Tacit recalled what he remembered about the rooms he had been in. They were all empty. But there was a milk cellar connected to the scullery, and there were some extra rooms on the other side of the house at the far end of the proper entrance, and some bedrooms off the big living room. You had to go outside to enter those. They had their own entrance.

He had to go look.

And was the money going to just lie here out in the open?

Tacit had to get hold of himself not to be panicked. What was happening to him since finding those coins? He almost didn't recognize himself anymore. Why was that happening? Those coins had been in the ground for about three hundred years.

But, he thought in his defense, things changed as soon as he knew they were there. And there were so many. He had to force himself to let the coins lie there while he crept down and found something to put them in. Who was going to coincidentally come up here where no one ever came? Ælgar with his stiff leg? Granny with her bad knees? Malvina? You are crazy, he mumbled to himself.

The door to the milk cellar had sunk. It hadn't been opened in years, and Tacit had to lift and wrestle with it for a while before he could scrape it open across the stone floor in the scullery. Behind the door, a black windowless cellar hole was revealed, with a stair made of large stones leading down into an abyss. Tacit hesitated. It was not very inviting. There could be anything down there.

"You sure are making a lot of noise," yelled Granny from the kitchen.

Tacit walked into the kitchen, found a stump of candle, and put a twig in through the stove lid to light it.

'What are you doing?" asked the old woman.

"Nothing," answered Tacit.

"Then why is it so noisy?"

"It's just the door," he said. "It hasn't been opened in a hundred years."

"The door."

"To the milk cellar. I'm just walking around looking at the

house."

She didn't believe him. She knew him too well for that. But he was an adult now; he would have to take care of himself. He had been bringing her half of his apprentice pay for a long time. She would have to leave him alone.

Tacit walked out with his candle and slowly made his way down the worn steps and looked around. It was a rather large room that extended a ways under the house. It had evidently been used as a larder as well as a milk cellar. Next to the steps were collapsed broad shelving for vats of milk. And the floor was full of shards from the crockery they hadn't taken with them, which had fallen to the ground along with the shelving.

He held the candle out to all sides. By the longest wall stood a salting basin carved out of a huge tree trunk, still with the lid on. And by the inner end wall were other shelves, where some were still in place with pickling jars and crocks still on them.

Afraid that the shelves would collapse when he touched them, Tacit carefully lifted the items from the shelves and carried them up to the scullery floor. Large and small crocks nesting inside one another and jelly jars, some still with a brownish-black substance on the bottom. On the floor below stood large stoneware, with plates tied on top. Tacit brought them upstairs as they were, and soon the whole floor in front of the stairs was covered with what he had found. Everything they had left behind.

They couldn't have brought it all with them, even if they wanted to, he thought. But it was usable. The Water Farm didn't have many household items, and nothing at all for keeping food.

He took a suitably-sized crock, walked out with it to the trough, and filled it with water so it could soak. Then he went and opened the kitchen door.

"Come look."

Both Granny and Malvina came carrying their sewing, and burst out in surprise at what he had found.

"All the shelves down there are totally rotten," he said, "and many of them have collapsed. But these can be used, can't they?" He poked at a jar with the tip of his shoe.

"My goodness, sure they can," said Granny happily. She immediately started to explain to Malvina how to clean them and then sterilize them in the copper kettle.

Malvina nodded, overwhelmed.

"I'll come and help you with it," Granny said, when she saw the girl's disheartened expression. "They can just stay there till when you have time. For now you'd better keep sewing."

Malvina sent her a look of gratitude, while Tacit began moving jars and crocks to the corner behind the copper kettle, so he could shut the door to the milk cellar again. He was surprised as well. The Water Farm was still holding onto secrets.

Outside by the water trough he started to clean his jar. He scraped out the decomposed contents and scrubbed it with sand and a clump of grass until all the brown was gone and the original gray surface emerged. Then he laid it to dry in the sun.

While the jar dried he wandered around restlessly, looking for the best place to bury it. Over in the garden; in the chicken yard; behind the barn where there was once a manure pile— but none of these places suited him. For a while he considered bringing the jar with the money in it back to the living room and putting it back underneath the floor there. But in the end he decided on the former garden. And when the jar was dry enough and he had put the coins inside it, he removed a piece of turf, and dug a hole big enough for the jar. Then he replaced the grass. The leftover dirt he threw out to the sides so there was no trace.

Then what?

The thought of the buried treasure would not leave him in peace. The next day he worked like a maniac in the smithy to alleviate his nervousness and restlessness. But it didn't work.

He continually questioned himself as to whether he was doing the right thing. What should he do with the money? What could he do?

Put them in the bank in town?

But would they take money that you couldn't use?

Buy a new house for Granny?

You couldn't do that either with money like that. And besides, she didn't want to move. But then what?

And where would he say he got them? No one would believe that he just found them. And in one way or another it seemed like a kind of dishonesty that he had just dug them out from under the floor at the Water Farm. Deep inside he knew that he was acting as if he had stolen them.

But was it stealing? Did they belong to someone? Whoever had buried them had been dead such a long time, there was no way you could find out who it was.

What if they weren't worth anything?

Tacit remembered the second-hand dealer where had once tried to sell his cast figurines. Maybe the dealer could tell him what they were worth.

Or Teacher Melin?

Tacit considered what would happen if he asked Melin and showed him a couple of coins. Melin knew a lot about old things, antiques and things like that. Melin would probably get all excited about it.

But what if a whole bunch of people came looking for more? What would happen to Ælgar and little Mina? And Malvina for that matter?

Granny observed him with worry. He had been so restless lately. What was plaguing him? What had he gotten himself into? He didn't answer when she asked, but by the way he tossed and turned at night, she judged it must be something serious. It was obvious just by looking at him.

Tacit fluctuated between Melin and the second-hand dealer.

The little old man with the thin spectacles on his nose who wouldn't believe he had made the figurines himself. Tacit never sold him anything, partly because of the dealer's suspiciousness, and partly because the blacksmith had forbidden him to make any more. But now he was almost a full blacksmith, and anyway, this was about old coins, which was completely different. Or was it? Would the second-hand dealer just believe that he had stolen the coins?

Tacit decided that he didn't trust the dealer's integrity. So he chose to go first to Teacher Melin.

That night, he slept.

And the next evening he went to see his old teacher and knocked on the door. Melin himself answered and looked pleasantly surprised at the sight of Tacit, but also a bit worried. Was there something wrong? It was the first time Tacit had visited him since the blacksmith had told Tacit that the female centaur was obscene.

"Come in, come in," said Teacher Melin, moving aside.

Tacit stepped in and noticed to his amazement that he was now taller than his teacher.

"I'd like to talk with you," he began solemnly.

"Then let us go into my office," answered Melin, who perceived something was going on.

He seated Tacit and then sat waiting at his desk. Tacit had a hard time getting started.

"Should I ask Helene to make some coffee?" asked Melin, so the silence wouldn't be too awkward.

Tacit shook his head.

"I'm not sure where to begin," he said, "but before I say anything, I have to make sure that this doesn't go any further."

"Of course," promised Melin, lighting his pipe.

"I'm afraid I've found a silver treasure," Tacit blurted out.

"A silver treasure?" repeated Melin astonished.

Tacit nodded.

"Well that's no catastrophe." Melin smiled, relieved.

"Maybe not, but it could easily become one, if I do the wrong thing," said Tacit seriously.

"Tell me about it. What kind of a silver treasure?"

"You know the Water Farm?" Tacit looked at him apprehensively; of course he knew the Water Farm.

"Sure. The place out by the beach? Where the old man lives? I've heard that you go out there."

"I help him out once in a while," said Tacit. "He's very lonely. He thinks everyone hates him because he served time for murder."

"They probably do," said Melin.

"But they're wrong. He never murdered anyone," answered Tacit.

"But he served his punishment."

"That doesn't make you a murderer. And that's not what this is about anyway. But he has a little three-year-old girl living there with him."

"Dear God." Melin was startled. "Is that working out?"

"Actually it is. He is both mother and father and a grandfather to her, and she is very bonded to him."

"Whose child is it?"

"Once he came upon a woman about to give birth by the side of the road, and he didn't know what to do with her so he took her back to the farm and put her in his bed. Then he went and got me and Granny, and Granny helped the baby be born. The woman lived through the winter on the Water Farm, but when the child was four or five months old she left. She disappeared and we haven't seen her since."

"That's terrible." Teacher Melin seemed shaken.

"That's what happened," said Tacit.

"And then the old man just kept the child?"

"He has been a better mother to her than the woman who gave birth to her. The girl is happy and healthy and Granny gets clothes for her or sews them herself."

"But should that continue?" asked Melin cautiously.

"It would kill him if someone came and took her away," said Tacit aggressively. "And the girl would suffer irreparable harm."

"Really? It couldn't be that bad."

"Yes it could," answered Tacit. "That's why I need your absolute silence about it. The old man knows that people think he's a murderer and he wouldn't stand a chance, if someone heard about the child. But I know that he took the punishment to protect the woman he loved who carried his child. For the sake of his son, he's made peace with the fact that she married another man while he was in prison."

Melin sat digesting all he had heard, and Tacit paused his story.

Then Melin said, "And now you've found a silver treasure?"

"I'm not really sure. I stepped through the floor in one of the rooms and down below there was a big pile of old coins."

That shook up Teacher Melin.

"How many," he just about whispered. He wasn't completely sitting down anymore.

"I haven't counted them," answered Tacit, "but there's a lot. And they're all different, big and small. I can't make out the letters on them, but on one of them it says 1564. Do you think they can still be used?"

"Did you bring any of them with you?" asked Teacher Melin breathless.

Tacit shook his head. "I wanted to speak with you first."

"Where are they?"

"I can't tell you. First I want to know what happens when someone finds something like that."

"Well, it's national treasure."

"What does that mean?"

"They have to be turned in."

"To who?"

"The authorities."

"And then what will happen?"

"You might get a finder's fee."

"It sounds like I should have kept my mouth shut."

"But you don't have the right to hold onto something like that," said Melin soberly.

"Okay, but no one knows about it but me."

"Well I do," said Melin with emphasis.

"It sounds like you would force me to turn them in."

"I would rather that you did it yourself."

"I get the feeling I would get more for them if I sold them little by little in town," Tacit said softly.

Melin straightened up with a jerk. "What are you saying? It's national treasure!"

Tacit shrugged. "I'm a fool," he said.

"I will send them to search the place if you try that," Melin exclaimed.

"You won't find anything anyway."

"I won't? I could go and find an unregistered child."

Tacit slumped in his chair. "That's blackmail," he said.

"The law is the law and it must be followed," responded Melin, suddenly feeling in control.

Tacit sat quietly and considered.

Then he said, "I don't want anyone out at the Water Farm. That's my price for turning it in."

"Well the place it was found has to be searched, that's for sure."

"What if I didn't find the coins there?" Tacit looked steadily and openly at Teacher Melin. The conversation had turned completely different than he had expected. Instead of an accomplice he had gained an opponent.

Melin seemed confused. "But didn't you say–?" he began.

"I'm not that dumb," laughed Tacit. "Do you think I want someone digging up the ground before I've had a chance to look for myself and see if there's any more? Do we have a deal?" He stood up.

Teacher Melin stood up too.

"If I can get hold of a man from a museum, will you meet him here with the coins?"

Tacit thought about it. "Okay," he said.

"What will you do with the money, when you get your reward?"

"I'm not really sure. Maybe buy the Water Farm."

"Is it for sale?" asked Melin, taken by surprise.

Tacit shrugged his shoulders. "I don't even know who owns it," he answered. "It would never be enough money anyway—not this way."

"You never know. It is pretty dilapidated."

"It can't really be used for anything," answered Tacit. "There's no land except the hole it's in."

"And you still might use your finder's fee on it?"

The thought spread inside Tacit like a wildfire. "He probably doesn't even live around here—the owner," he said.

"Maybe I could find out for you," offered Teacher Melin hesitatingly.

"That couldn't do any harm," said Tacit.

They walked to the foyer.

"What will you do with the girl when she has to go to school?" asked Melin suddenly.

Tacit lifted his head. "We'll figure it out," he said. "A lot can happen between now and then."

"He could die—the old man?"

"That too, sure. He's not young anymore."

"You've always done things your own way," said Teacher Melin with a shallow sigh.

"Thanks," answered Tacit, and he stepped out onto the street.

Doubt and Determination

Tacit had a bad conscience because he had revealed little Mina's presence at the Water Farm to Teacher Melin. It felt like he had gone behind old Ælgar's back. But at the same time he didn't think he had a choice. If he had shown Ælgar the coins, he would have demanded they be put back where they were found—or he would have found a way to pour them out into a peat pit just to get rid of them. Ælgar wanted to preserve his solitude. His fear of strangers had not diminished with the years.

If only Teacher Melin would keep his word and not reveal what he now knew.

Tacit assured himself again and again that of course Melin would keep his word, but at the same time, doubt and fear ate at him. He knew his old teacher well enough to know that he was very interested in antiquities, and the possibility of a genuine silver treasure could completely disconcert him to the extent that he might forget himself.

And when Tacit stood in the smithy, cut off from the world around him by his own hammer blows, he repeated for himself the conversation with Teacher Melin—what was said, which words were chosen, the tone that was used. He sought the vulnerable places, where something might have been misunderstood. And every time he arrived at Melin's question about what he would do with the finder's fee, he paused.

"Buy the Water Farm," he had answered.

It made him wonder every time. It wasn't something he had thought about beforehand. The words just spilled out. And it wasn't until later he realized that was the only right way to spend the money. The more he thought it over, the more right it seemed. Strange he never thought about it before.

But would a finder's fee be enough to buy a farm? It was true he had said to Melin that it was pretty worthless. All the buildings were dilapidated and the small amount of land that was left was sloping so much it couldn't be farmed. And besides, there was still the danger of another flood. The Water Farm ought to cost nearly nothing.

But he also knew that as soon as there was interest in an object, the object increased in value.

Regardless, the desire to buy the Water Farm took hold inside him. And he started thinking about other ways of raising the money. The first thing that occurred to him was to sell Granny's house and move her to the Water Farm; but that was also the least likely. He would never be able to convince her to part with the house where Mikkel had been born and had lived his whole life, and where she had lived with him since they were married, until his death.

And his half of his apprentice salary wouldn't be enough.

But what if he tried again with the second-hand dealer who was interested in the figurines he had made? That deal had fallen through because the man insisted that Tacit must have stolen them, and Tacit was too proud to let himself be regarded as a thief. All the figurines still lay wrapped in cloth in his room at Granny's.

If the dealer bought them, then maybe the blacksmith would give him permission to make more of them at the smithy after work.

Tacit thought it over. And since there was never long from thought to action with him, he spoke with the blacksmith and asked for time off to go to town that afternoon.

The second-hand dealer didn't recognize him. Tacit had changed from a lanky boy to a grown young man, and the little gray shopkeeper with the round steel spectacles on his nose didn't know what Tacit was referring to. It wasn't until Tacit unrolled the figurines from their cloth wrapping that the dealer realized who he was speaking with. He remembered Tacit the boy quite well.

Immediately the dealer pulled him into the back room.

"So it's you." He looked Tacit up and down, impressed that the boy had grown a head taller than himself. "Do you still insist that you made these yourself?" he asked quietly, picking up one of the apostles in his hand.

"You can believe whatever you want, as far as I care," answered Tacit. "I haven't changed my mind. The question is whether you want to buy them from me."

The dealer hesitated, but Tacit got the distinct impression that he was interested.

"How much would you pay for the one in your hand?" asked Tacit.

The man looked at him sideways. Tacit had decided before he left home that he wanted to get as much as possible for his figurines.

"Well," said the dealer, taking off his glasses and holding the figurine up close to his eyes. Then he took out a loupe and examined it carefully. Tacit thought he was stalling. The dealer glanced intermittently at Tacit's rural clothing. Then he threw out a price to try and catch Tacit off guard.

But all the dealer's tricks told Tacit the price was too low. The country boy inside him was supposed to be bowled over, and it was more money than he could have imagined in his wildest fantasy. He didn't have any experience negotiating prices in town, but he had been at the market and seen how salesmen haggled over horses and cows; so he knew that at all costs he had to hide what he was feeling.

Back when he had been in with his figurines the first time, he would have happily parted with them for a third the price. Immediately he began rolling up the small men in their cloths again.

But when he reached for the last apostle, which the dealer

was still holding, the dealer raised the price by twenty-five percent.

Tacit looked at him intently.

"That sounds more reasonable," he said. And then he added on some more so the price was half again as high as the first offer.

The dealer squirmed.

"But then you have to bring me all the ones you can get," he said.

"You have my word," said Tacit, laying the figurines back down on the table near them.

The little gray man counted the amount out in bills and handed them to Tacit, who felt like he ought to count them, even though he hadn't finished multiplying the price by the number of pieces. Without lifting his head he looked questioningly under his brow at the dealer, who handed him a couple of coins with an almost inaudible sigh. Tacit stuck it all in his pocket and started home.

Each figurine had brought him as much money as he earned in a whole week at the smithy. Still he was pretty sure that the little man with the mousey movements was going to make money on the deal. There must be someone who would pay a lot for that kind of thing.

Tacit felt relief in his body and an urge to run and skip. But he walked like he always did. There was no reason to invite people to ask problematic questions.

It was late in the evening by the time he reached his village. Still he stopped at the smithy, where the blacksmith had been nice enough to let him have the afternoon off. Tacit met the blacksmith outside, where he was standing with both hands buried in his pockets and his head back, as he often would stand when checking on the weather before going in to bed.

The blacksmith instinctively turned his head and cleared his throat in greeting when he saw Tacit stopping at the hedge.

This was a strange time to be coming by.

"So?" he said, as if expecting some difficulty. There were some days he wished he'd never taken that headstrong boy as an apprentice way back when. But at the same time he was fearful of the day Tacit would come and say that he didn't want to work there any more. Then what would he do? The boy was talented and he was a hard worker.

Tacit was not intimidated by the blacksmith's dismissive attitude: he got straight to the point.

"Do you mind if I make something in the smithy after work?" he asked.

"Do you have to come bothering me with questions like that in the middle of the night?" asked the blacksmith in reply.

"Well, it's not all that dark yet," said Tacit, "and you're still out."

The blacksmith waited.

Then he asked Tacit, "What are you going to make?"

"Saints."

"Saints?" The blacksmith squeezed his eyes half shut. "Like the ones you made a few years ago?"

"Right. Like them. Little saints." Tacit sounded optimistic.

The blacksmith hesitated. "But there will be no filth with four arms and stuff like that," he said.

"You can easily check them yourself," answered Tacit relaxed. "You can come over and see what I'm making." The blacksmith's house was no more than a few steps from the smithy, with just a bit of yard and a gravel pad between them.

The blacksmith grumbled.

"What are you going to make them out of?" he asked.

"Tin, brass, or maybe bronze. I don't know what I can get my hands on. I'll have to experiment—with the casts, too." Tacit's blood flowed warm and free, and his voice was eager and confident. He felt the future was something within his reach.

"Well how did you make the others—back then?"

"I cut them out of wax first, as precisely as I could. I tried with sheep tallow too, but that didn't work so well—it's not flexible enough—it breaks off in flakes too easily."

"Sheep tallow?" mumbled the blacksmith with disgust.

"Yeah. Granny was furious when I did it. Then I packed the wax figures in a thick covering of clay, so there was only a tiny hole at the bottom of the feet, and I let them dry. When they were dry enough I melted the wax out of the cavity."

"In the forge?"

"No, home in Granny's stove."

"What about the wax?"

"It burned up, of course. I didn't know how to save it."

"Then you poured molten tin into the hole?"

"Yeah. Or brass." I did that here in the smithy. But I had to fix them a lot. It took just as long to file and polish a figure as it took to cut it out of the wax. And the clay covering broke apart into too many pieces to be able to be reused. So I have some things to figure out."

"Right," said the blacksmith. "I'm going in. Goodnight." He left quickly, so he wouldn't get involved in any more explanations.

"Goodnight," said Tacit, resignedly. He wanted to hear what the blacksmith knew about casting, but obviously the man wasn't interested in talking.

There was a light in the office at Teacher Melin's place, so Tacit walked through the yard and knocked carefully on the glass with the tip of his finger. Shortly thereafter, the window was opened.

"Who's there?"

Tacit answered that it was him.

"Is something wrong?"

Tacit could tell by Melin's voice that he was thinking about the coins.

"No," he answered. "I just wanted to ask if you had a book."

"Something particular?"

"Do you have anything about casting?"

"You already borrowed that one."

"You don't have any others?"

"No."

"Then I'd like to borrow that same one again. It's been a long time since I had it."

Melin moved away from the window and came back with a fat volume, which stood out against the backlighting.

"What are you going to cast?" asked Melin, keeping the book up in the windowsill.

"Figurines."

"There's no chance you're planning to melt those coins, is there?" Melin's voice bore his somber premonition out through the window opening.

"No," answered Tacit outside in the dark.

"That would be a punishable offense," came the warning down from the opening.

"Yes, I figured."

"Here." Melin handed him the book. "You should have gotten a degree," he said. "You should have gone to school in the city—back then."

Tacit didn't answer. He just thanked him for the book and said goodnight.

The city school. Tacit made his way back to Granny's house. Teacher Melin had talked a lot about it back when Tacit got confirmed and finished elementary school. Several times Melin had gone out to visit Granny and pointed out that the boy ought to stay in school. The old woman received his message with reservations and discomfort. No one in their family had ever gone on to study before. They all worked.

Tacit hadn't been interested anyway. He wasn't attracted to the city. And since they had no money to board him at school either, the issue faded away on its own. He couldn't attend a place like that in hand-me-downs and patched clothing, and not in clogs, either.

Tacit walked home to Granny's kitchen and sat down to read with both his elbows on the table, even though it was already late. He was smoldering and boiling inside with everything his meeting with the dealer had set in motion. He saw a great opportunity before him.

The next morning when Granny came out to the kitchen, he was still sitting there, with his head on his arm on top of the book, sleeping.

"Goodness, boy," she exclaimed, startled. "Haven't you been to bed?"

Tacit lifted his drowsy head and looked around, bewildered.

"You're going to cost me a fortune in kerosene at this rate," gently scolded the old woman, moving the burned-out lamp back to the nail on the wall.

"We'll get more," mumbled Tacit, stretching himself out of his uncomfortable position.

"How?"

"I'm going to turn it into money."

"That's a cock and bull story if I ever heard one." Granny left no doubt about what she thought, as she shuffled out to the pantry to cut some bread.

"You don't believe me?" Tacit raised his voice so it would reach her.

"I'm not sure what I do or don't. At any rate I haven't seen much of that yet," came a somewhat distant reply.

"Then come in here and see." Tacit stuck his hand in his pocket.

"What should I come and see?" Granny didn't seem very interested when she returned carrying bread, lard and jelly.

"This here." Tacit lifted his arm and let the bills from the previous day fall like dry leaves onto the kitchen table.

"My dear Lord." Granny just about dropped the lard crock from sheer astonishment. "What's this all about?"

"Money," laughed Tacit.

"Where did you get it from?" Her tone was sharp.

"I earned it," he laughed.

"Earned it how?" Granny didn't know what to believe. "You got it legally, I assume."

"Do you remember the small men I made just after I became the blacksmith's apprentice?"

"What about them?" Granny expected the worst.

"I sold them."

"And then what?"

"Well that's how I got all this money."

"Right. Try and convince me of that. That much money for some little trinkets –."

"But it's true."

Granny didn't believe him. "You'd better hurry up and eat or you're going to be late." She placed the jelly glass down hard and put the bread down next to it. Then she lit the Primus stove and started water for coffee.

"Here's money for kerosene," said Tacit, pushing one of the bills over towards her.

"No way. I'm not buying kerosene with that kind of money."

Tacit sighed and rose heavily, stiff in his back and neck from sleeping on the table.

"You have always been so stubborn," he mumbled, walking into his room briefly, before re-emerging with a bill just like the other one.

"Here," he said. "I earned this one at the smithy. This one might work better for buying kerosene."

Granny mumbled something evasive down into her coffee funnel, but she let the bill remain inside her apron pocket where he had placed it.

"But there's nothing wrong with the sale I made," explained

Tacit, spreading marmalade thickly on his bread. "The second-hand dealer can resell those figurines—and make money on them. Otherwise he wouldn't have bought them. If anyone has gotten cheated it would be me."

Granny didn't answer. She remembered well how unbearable he had been back when he was working on those figurines, but he was always like that when he had something going on.

When Tacit had left, Granny collected all the bills and smoothed them out and laid them in his dresser under his clean underwear, where he usually kept his extra money. He was a good boy; she knew that. There was just so much about him she didn't understand. He got so many strange ideas—like all the mess when he sat at her kitchen table carving wax figures, and the scraps that got tramped into the floor so she had to lie there, scraping it with a knife to get them off again—and she mustn't touch anything or move anything before he was done. Good riddance to all his castings. But that he could get that much money for such worthless things!

Over at the smithy, the blacksmith glanced uneasily at his apprentice who was going at his work as if it were an enemy he had to personally defeat. With a serious expression and even more silently than usual, Tacit concentrated on his project. Was it because he wanted to do a bit more since he had taken off the afternoon before? Or was there something bothering him? The blacksmith didn't know what to think. It was almost too good to be true. He almost started feeling lonely.

"Is something bothering you?" he asked cautiously when they had reached lunchtime and Tacit hadn't said a word other than good morning.

"What?" asked Tacit, looking up.

"You look like you've been stood up by a girl. You have never lived up to your name better than you have today."

"Sorry about that. I just keep thinking about that casting

form. I wonder if I could make them out of clay in two halves so they could be opened and used again. Or if I could use sand."

The blacksmith pushed his cap down in front on his forehead and scratched himself in the back of the neck. "How many did you plan on making?" he asked.

"Lots of them. As many as I can."

"Small holy men?"

"I told you last night." Tacit sounded impatient.

"Are you planning to start a whole foundry?"

"I'm going to need some money," admitted Tacit.

"I figured that. How much?"

"I don't know yet."

"Is she pregnant?" asked the blacksmith trying to catch him off guard.

"Who?" asked Tacit, surprised.

"I thought maybe you knocked someone up," mumbled the blacksmith, retreating apologetically.

"What made you think that?" asked Tacit.

"When that happens people need money."

"Well—well it's not that."

Tacit didn't tell him what it was, which the blacksmith thought he could have done, since he was letting him use the smithy in the evenings.

The blacksmith's mood did not improve when Teacher Melin came by at five o'clock, said something to Tacit, and then disappeared with only a quick nod to the blacksmith. And as soon as he had left, Tacit said that he had to leave.

"There's still an hour till six o'clock." stated the blacksmith.

"I know," answered Tacit, "but I have to."

"You could just finish that piece you're working on first."

"No, I can't," said Tacit and put down what he was holding. With no further explanation he went and washed off the worst of the filth in the water trough next to the forge. The blacksmith scowled at him as he walked out.

When he got close enough that he could see over the roofs of the Water Farm he stopped short. Down below in the bed he had dug, Malvina was making holes with a short branch and, following behind her, little Mina was putting potatoes into the holes. Comfort-child lay in a nest of straw at the end of the bed.

Tacit couldn't help but wonder if he was about to ruin what old Ælgar was trying to create. He walked slowly down the wheel track that almost wasn't a wheel track anymore. Yellow Ingelin was nowhere to be seen on the sloping grass, but if Ælgar wasn't home, that was a good thing.

Malvina stood up quickly when she heard him.

"Oh, it's you," she said, when she saw who it was. "You haven't been here in quite a while."

"There's been a lot going on," he said apologetically and walked over to Mina.

"You're planting potatoes?" He smiled at her.

She nodded solemnly.

"You're helping Malvina?"

"Yes." answered the child.

"I found a bag of them in the corner of the utility room," answered Malvina.

"Oh, right." Tacit remembered.

"If you had said something we could have planted them a long time ago."

"I forgot all about them," said Tacit. "I was going to plant them myself." He looked with acknowledgment from her to the potato bed.

"You raked it," he said.

"I did that a while ago," she answered.

"You're feeling better."

Malvina looked away self-consciously.

"I've never been anywhere better than here," she said.

"Will you make some coffee?" he asked.

Malvina hesitated.

"How do you know I have coffee?"

"Because most of what Granny had back home suddenly disappeared," laughed Tacit. "Will you make some?"

Malvina nodded. She walked over and picked up Comfort.

"We can sit on the back steps," he suggested. "I have to leave again soon. I'm going to visit Teacher Melin tonight."

Disappointment clouded her expression, and he sat down on the stoop with Mina while Malvina went inside.

Shortly afterwards Malvina called for Mina, and the child went in and returned with three cups, one with a bit of milk in it. Behind her came Malvina with three slices of freshly baked bread on the cutting board and coffee in a milk pitcher in the other hand.

"What about the little one?" asked Tacit.

"She fell asleep," answered Malvina and sat down.

"You have butter!" exclaimed Tacit when he saw the bread had been spread.

"I made it myself. It's goat butter. It gives enough that I can take off the cream."

Tacit was impressed.

"Where did you learn to do that?"

"Nowhere. I just figured it out."

Tacit took a bit of bread and complimented her on it. Then they just sat for a while.

"Tell me about the woman who wanted you to stay with her," he asked.

Malvina hesitated.

"Maybe another day," she said softly. "You have to go to Teacher Melin tonight."

"Just a little bit?" he asked again.

She shook her head, and he knew it was because he hadn't been there for so long.

"You're right," he agreed. "I have to go home and get cleaned up and change my clothes. But I'll be back soon. Then I'll take you to the beach."

"Will you?"

Tacit felt a bit of longing behind her words which warmed him inside.

"Yes," he promised. "I will."

He thanked her for the coffee, got up, and left. He went back across the courtyard and the opposite way around the farmhouse to the place where he had buried the coins. Carefully he lifted the piece of turf and removed the jar from the hole.

Nielsen-Snook

Granny was pestering him. She always did this when she felt he was involved in something he was keeping from her. Fear that he would get caught up in something bad never left her, and the feeling increased when she could tell he was being secretive.

Tacit wolfed down his food. He was going to skip getting washed, but Granny forced him, and demanded that he put on nice clothes too.

"Helene Melin is very particular about things like that," she explained. "And I don't want it hanging over my head that you are dirtying people's furniture when you go visit them."

Tacit felt defensive. Everything had taken longer than he thought it would, and it was his own doing—going to the farm and getting Malvina to make coffee. She thought it had been a long time between his visits, but he had been preoccupied with so many other things. He didn't know how to get her to understand that. She didn't know about his figurines—or the treasure—not yet.

When Tacit finally made it to the schoolhouse it was quite a bit later than Teacher Melin had said, and he saw Melin pacing uneasily in front of the lamplight in the office. A huge shadow—first one direction and then the other. Melin was afraid that Tacit wasn't going to show up, that something went wrong and that he had alerted the man from the museum in vain. But Granny was not easy to dodge. She had set a large tub in the scullery and heated an extra kettle of water while he ate. She laid out clean underwear and his Sunday clothes on the scullery counter without even acknowledging Tacit's insistence that he was already late.

While he had been getting washed, Tacit had thought about

Malvina and the kitchen at the Water Farm, which was cleaner than it had ever been in all the times he'd been there. Neither Ælgar nor he himself had given it much thought; they just used it the way it was. And Gunhilda was preoccupied with her future in some other place; she had only done what was absolutely necessary while waiting until she could leave. It was never her kitchen in the way it was becoming Malvina's.

"Where have you been!" exclaimed Teacher Melin as he let Tacit in. "We've been sitting here waiting for you, wondering if something terrible had happened to you. It could be unsafe walking the roads carrying valuables."

Tacit apologized for his tardiness and quickly handed the jar to Melin to avoid having to explain where he had been. Teacher Melin marched into his office with the prize in his outstretched hands as if it had been a reliquary at the front of a procession.

Inside the office a serious man stood up from his chair. It was apparent that he had come a long way, and Tacit understood how embarrassed the teacher must have felt about having him sit there, waiting.

The man greeted Tacit reservedly, exuding a sense of importance.

"Nielsen-Snook," he said. "With a hyphen."

Tacit felt a bit uncomfortable with the man's ceremonious manner, but if it had to be that way, then –

"Mortensen," he said, reaching out his hand. At that moment he was thankful to Granny for making him bathe and put on clean clothes.

Melin handed the jar to Nielsen-Snook with extreme humility. Nielsen-Snook received it with the fingertips of both hands, examining it closely, and even a bit myopically. It looked like he was trying to keep his hands from getting dirty.

"Strange," said the visitor, clearing his throat. "Didn't you say 1564?"

Tacit didn't answer, and Nielsen-Snook watched him closely,

over the top of the jar he was still holding up to his eyes.

"Are you sure you found them in this?"

"I just carried them here in that," answered Tacit, trying to be just as reserved as the stranger. "I found the coins in the ground."

"Well you could have said that to begin with."

"I never said anything about a jar; only about coins," answered Tacit.

"Are you saying they were lying loose in the ground?"

"Yes, I took them out of the ground."

"Where?"

"Underneath a big rock." Tacit didn't like the man's interrogatory tone. It made it sound as if he had committed a kind of robbery.

"With nothing holding them together?" said Nielsen-Snook.

"In the hole there was something that I thought was a dead, dried-out rat at first," said Tacit.

"You mean hide?"

"Yes, horsehide."

"How can you be so sure?" Suspicious, the man lifted his head.

"I'm a blacksmith. I've shoed a lot of horses. I know what horsehide looks like."

"Why didn't you bring that too?"

"I thought what mattered was the coins."

"I think now we should look at what's inside," interrupted Teacher Melin. He felt uncomfortable with the conflict building between Nielsen-Snook and Tacit, and he was afraid of where it might lead.

Without a word, Nielsen-Snook emptied the jar, leaving a large pile of coins mixed with dirt on Melin's desk. Tacit hadn't thought of cleaning out the dirt from the garden. He wouldn't have had time anyway.

"Oh my goodness," exclaimed the stranger when he saw

how many coins there were. "This is unbelievable." Eagerly he started fingering the coins and sorting them.

Teacher Melin went over to the other side of the desk and joined in the sorting from there. Within a few moments they were so absorbed by the old coins they completely forgot that Tacit was still in the room. He sat there all the while, attempting to understand what they meant by what they said, but there were too many words he didn't know. The only thing he was sure of was that he had brought something significant.

Completely engrossed, the two men laid the coins on a sheet of clean, white paper and sorted them by type and size. Eventually only the dirt was spread across the papers that had been lying there. Melin walked out and returned with a brush and dustpan.

While Melin swept up, Nielsen-Snook counted the coins, both the ones he had sorted and the ones Melin had sorted.

"Amazing," said Nielsen-Snook, astounded. "We'll be famous when they find out about this."

"So can I leave now?" asked Tacit, rising from his chair.

"Yes. Mortensen can leave." Nielsen-Snook didn't even look up when he answered.

Tacit remained standing.

"I'd like a receipt," he said.

They both stared, open-mouthed, at Tacit. "A receipt?"

"With both the number and the total weight of the coins," he said.

"But a receipt? Why would you want that?"

"So I'll know what I delivered and to whom," Tacit said.

"Well, we can't just do that," exclaimed Nielsen-Snook. "We never do that."

"And you'll get your finder's fee," said Melin, trying to smooth things over.

"Yes, I'm counting on that too," said Tacit, making no sign of leaving.

Somewhat reluctantly, Teacher Melin went out and brought back his wife's kitchen scale. He put the coins on the scale while the other wrote down the amounts, signed the paper, and handed it to Tacit.

"We'll come out and look at the site of origin tomorrow," said Nielsen-Snook, already shifting his focus back to the relics.

"No!" exclaimed Melin, alarmed.

"Sure we will. We always examine the site. We can't rule out that there could be more there."

"But that won't be so easy," said Melin nervously.

"And why can't we?" Nielsen-Snook turned around on his chair to look directly at Melin who still stood there, holding the brush and the full dustpan.

"Because…because…." Melin turned helplessly towards Tacit.

"That won't be any problem," said Tacit calmly.

Melin stared at him astonished.

"But you said…."

"I think that sounds fine," repeated Tacit.

"Where did you find them?" Nielsen-Snook spun around in his chair to look at Tacit. Then the man removed his lorgnette.

"Under a big rock near Eagle Hill."

"Eagle Hill, I see. And where is this Eagle Hill?"

"In Mads Nedergård's field just outside of town. Teacher Melin knows where it is."

"And what made you go there?" Tacit noticed the inquisitorial tone again, so he hesitated just long enough before answering, so the man would think Tacit was uncomfortable about telling him.

"I took a girl up there. No one ever goes up there."

"And then you found all the coins?"

"No. There was a fox that had dug underneath a rock. The coins were in the dirt it threw out."

"When was that?"

"It's some time ago." Tacit stole a glance over at Teacher Melin, who was thunderstruck by how easy it was for Tacit to lie.

"And who was the girl you had with you?"

"No. That's going too far. My girlfriends don't matter in this." Even though it was a lie, Tacit felt encroached upon.

"But maybe she could have taken some of the coins?"

"I would like Teacher Melin to vouch for the girl," said Tacit, turning toward his teacher. Melin had regained his composure enough that he could ensure, in any case, that the girl hadn't taken anything that wasn't hers.

"You know her?"

"I can vouch for her."

"Fine. So we agree that Mortensen will lead us to the site of origin," concluded Nielsen-Snook.

Tacit made no answer, but said goodnight and walked quickly out through the school hallway and out to the yard. While he hurried in the direction of Granny's house, he thought that if he had known what kind of person would be handling the case, he probably would have decided to keep the coins and melt them down.

Granny was already in bed. He took the kitchen clock into his room and set the alarm to go off at four o'clock. Even as Nielsen-Snook was asking in his offensive, cutting way, Tacit was already making his plan. Waking up early was imperative. Already at the first ring his hand was on the clock. He snuck out and put on his work clothes which still lay in the scullery. Then he left the house and walked towards the Water Farm.

The sun had barely made it out of the morning clouds by the time he reached the little courtyard by the spring. He tried the scullery door and found it unlocked. The door to the kitchen wasn't latched either, and it opened without too much creaking. The next door to the old sitting room was noisier, but Tacit kept an eye on Malvina, sleeping on the bed with both children, and she didn't move. Then he snuck into the empty room and through to the great room.

The "rat corpse" still lay where he had left it. He pushed it a bit further into the room and then stepped deliberately on the rotted board ends, to break them off around the hearth's foundation.

He gathered the wooden pieces into a pile so he could see the dirt below. Here he began searching in earnest. With his bare hands he scooped up the dirt and placed it on the wooden floor, where it quickly accumulated into four brown-black piles. He reached further and further underneath the ashlar stones and all the way out to the edge of the floor. Then he knelt down next to the piles of dirt and started sifting through them by spreading them out a little at a time, before brushing the dirt back down where it came from.

He was so preoccupied that he didn't notice Malvina silently enter the room, and stand there, watching him in disbelief. She stood for a long while, wrapped in her pale woolen sheet, before he felt her gaze upon him and looked up.

He was startled at the sight of the white figure. He had just been sitting there thinking about the man who had hid his money under the stove long ago, and never had the chance to dig it up again. Then he saw that it was Malvina and he felt both sheepish and relieved.

"What are you doing?" she asked, without moving closer.

"I'm trying to keep you from becoming homeless," he answered.

She hesitated a moment.

Then she said, "What?"

Tacit repeated what he just said.

Malvina said sharply, "To me it looks like you're sitting there spreading dirt around on the floor."

"This is just the beginning," he answered, and kept working.

"Why are you doing that?"

"I'm looking for some coins."

"Money? In all that?" She didn't believe him.

Without a word Tacit pointed to three coins lying on a clean piece of flooring next to him.

Malvina came over and stared at them.

"Old ones like that—you can't use them for anything, can you?"

"Not for buying anything, but they're still useful."

"How can they keep me from becoming homeless?" she asked.

"Because I've gotten myself involved in something that looks like it was kind of dumb," he said, sighing.

"You haven't said anything about that before, have you?" Malvina gave him a questioning look. "Come into the kitchen and I'll make coffee. There's some bread from yesterday. Then you can tell me about it."

Tacit ran his fingers through the last bit of dirt and stood up. He swept the rest of the dirt into the hole with his foot. Then he bent down and picked up the coins.

"This is just what I needed," he said.

"Come on. I'll make some coffee," said Malvina.

"Thanks."

Tacit went out and washed the dirt off his hands and arms at the spring, and when he came back in she was already dressed and lighting the wood stove. Mina was sitting up in bed, rubbing her eyes sleepily.

"You can stay asleep," said Tacit. "It's not daytime yet."

"Yes it is. I want to be awake when you're here."

"Should I help you put on your clothes?" he asked, walking over to the bed.

"I can do it myself."

"You can? But then what will I do?"

"You can change Comfort. She's wet—all the way through."

"Do you think I can do that?" Tacit sounded unsure.

"If Grandpa can, then you can too. I'll tell you how." Mina stood up and took some clothes from the shelf over the bed.

"This is a diaper," she said. "And these are pants. And this is her wrap." She gave him what she had in her hands.

Tacit glanced at Malvina, but she was preoccupied with cutting bread.

"First you take off all the wet things," said Mina.

"Right," answered Tacit. "And in the meantime you put something on so you don't get cold."

Mina hopped down to the foot of the bed, found her clothes, and pulled her dress over her head. Then she turned back to Tacit and Comfort.

"What next?" he asked, standing with the clean diaper.

"You have to fold it into a triangle."

Tacit did as she said.

"Then you lift up her legs."

Tacit lifted them, and Mina laid the diaper under Comfort and folded it around her.

"Now you can put her pants on. That's hard," she said. She walked back to the foot of the bed and found her top. She put it on inside out.

"Nice. You are so smart," said Malvina from over at the table. She cut off Tacit from saying anything about the shirt. Then she filtered the coffee into the old milk pitcher and announced that coffee was ready. Tacit wrapped Comfort in her swaddling clothes and carried her to the table.

It was warm and cozy in the kitchen despite the early hour. The heat from the stove made the room inviting. Mina crept up and knelt on the bench. Then she turned expectantly towards Tacit.

"Butter a piece for me," she told him.

"What about Comfort?" he asked her.

"Nothing for her," said Mina.

"But how can I butter bread for you while I'm holding her?"

"Malvina can do it," announced the three-year-old child, laying a slice of bread in front of him on the table.

Malvina hid a smile and poured the coffee.

"Should I go and wake Ælgar?" she said.

"I don't think so. It's better if he doesn't find out just yet. He just gets all worked up."

Malvina placed a piece of dry bread in Comfort's fingers so the baby would have something to occupy herself with. Then she buttered a slice for herself. She watched Tacit lay Comfort on her belly across his lap to free up his hands. When he finished buttering Mina's bread, he sat Comfort up again.

"So tell us," said Malvina.

"It all started when I stepped through the floor that day I went into the great room," he said. "I wanted to look closer at the wood stove, and my foot went through. In the dirt I found a whole lot of old coins."

"Was that the day you were down in the milk cellar too?" asked Malvina.

"I was looking for something to put them in," said Tacit with a crooked smile.

He took a bite of bread and told how it had affected him to suddenly be responsible for a bunch of silver.

"Silver? Is it silver, those there?" She pointed at the coins he had laid on the table top.

"They are," he answered. "There were a hundred and twenty-six coins and they weighed almost two pounds."

"My goodness," Malvina blurted out. She looked thoroughly startled.

"I couldn't sleep that night because of it. What was I going to do with two pounds of silver that wasn't mine and that I didn't know who they belonged to?"

"And that's why you didn't come by all that time," said Malvina half to herself.

"That's right. Finally I went to Teacher Melin and told him

about it, and he just about hit the ceiling.

"He said it was 'national treasure,' and that it had to be turned in. I absolutely could not keep it myself—it would be a punishable offense."

"Punishable?"

"That's what he said. But he might have just said that to keep me from melting it down."

"But turned in?" said Malvina a bit disappointed. "Just turned in, just like that? When you're the one who found it?"

"He said I would get a finder's fee."

"But still. Two pounds of silver?" Malvina shook her head. "Who do you turn it in to?"

"The authorities, or the king, or a museum or something like that. I don't really know."

"So are you going to do it?"

"I already did."

She stared at him. "Why might that make me homeless?" she asked again.

"Because the blasted museum man is determined to examine the place I found them," answered Tacit.

"What does that have to do with me?"

"Can't you see what will happen if he comes here and starts digging around in that room? Half the parish will be out here poking around when they hear that someone found silver here. It would be like hanging a flag on the roof."

"And what about Ælgar and Mina?" said Malvina

"And what about you and Comfort? Everything would be ruined."

Malvina stared at him motionless.

"So what are you going to do?" she whispered.

"I'm going to make a new finding place. That's what I'm doing now. That's why I came to try and find some more coins."

"And what if he comes here anyway?" Malvina kept her eyes on Tacit.

"I told him I found the coins at Eagle Hill," said Tacit.

Malvina didn't respond.

"I'm going to make it look real before I go to work," he continued.

"With those coins?" she asked.

"Right, and with the piece of animal hide that's still lying in there." Tacit got up and handed Comfort to Malvina. "I have to go now," he said and walked in to get the piece of hide.

"I'll be back again soon." Tacit went to the door, then he turned around.

"He asked me why I was up on Eagle Hill," he said, looking right at Malvina.

"So?"

"I told him I was up there with a girl."

"Why are you telling me this?"

" Because I wanted you to know that it's not true, just in case you hear it from someone else."

Then he left.

EAGLE HILL

They came to pick up Tacit in the middle of the morning. Melin remained by the door while Nielsen-Snook continued striding vigorously into the half-dark abyss without a word. He stopped and peered around until he spotted Tacit standing by the forge. But he didn't recognize him in the different clothing. So Nielsen-Snook walked up to him and asked for Mortensen.

"Yes," answered Tacit hesitantly.

Nielsen-Snook recognized his voice and hid his mistake beneath an offended expression.

"You'd better come with us," he said.

"Has Mr. Nielsen asked Master?"

"Nielsen-Snook," corrected the museum man.

"Has Mr. Nielsen-Snook asked Master?" repeated Tacit obediently. He was having trouble remaining serious.

"Master? What master?" Nielsen-Snook looked around him in the wrong direction. And Tacit pointed out the blacksmith who Nielsen-Snook had just walked past.

"No. About what?" Nielsen-Snook turned around.

"I'm an apprentice. I can't go anywhere without permission," he explained.

The stranger took a couple of steps in the direction of the heavy-set, blackened man.

"We're just going to need him for a little while," he announced.

"Is that so?" said the blacksmith, interested. He dropped what he was working on and walked up to the museum man. "What has he done?"

Nielsen-Snook gave a perplexed expression.

"What do you mean 'done'?"

"Aren't you from the police?"

"No. Why would you think that?" Nielsen-Snook seemed a bit confused. He thought the blacksmith was standing much too close.

"Since you're just coming all the sudden and taking him."

Nielsen-Snook waved his hands dismissively.

"Not at all. Not at all," he assured him.

Nielsen-Snook seemed no less an outsider by the bright summer jacket he was wearing.

"Well, where are you taking him?" The blacksmith was eager to know.

"My good blacksmith," began the stranger, his voice dripping with the big city –

Holy Moses, thought Tacit, afraid the blacksmith would get riled up by being spoken to like that. But the blacksmith just waited for him to finish.

"The issue is that the young man there has turned in a silver treasure he found."

The blacksmith spun around and speared Tacit with a pair of incredulous eyes.

"Aha, so that's the calamity. And where did you happen to find it?"

"On Eagle Hill," answered Tacit.

The blacksmith's eyes narrowed.

"Then it wasn't that far from what I had said," he inferred. "It did have something to do with a girl, didn't it?"

Tacit grinned. The blacksmith's reaction fit like a glove with his own explanation.

"Well, let's go," said Nielsen-Snook.

Tacit didn't move.

"What does Master say?" he asked.

"Listen, this is about national treasure!" yelled the stranger suddenly. "We can't stay here all day. We have to get a move on!"

"You're a national treasure," mumbled the blacksmith.

Nielsen-Snook didn't hear him. He was already moving towards the door.

"You never told me where you were taking him," said the blacksmith to the man's back.

"To Eagle Hill, of course," the bright jacket responded, in an irritated voice.

"Hmm. So this won't take all day?" asked the blacksmith towards Tacit.

"No," said Tacit.

Then they left. Teacher Melin walked beside Nielsen-Snook and Tacit walked beside Melin, so they filled the roadway. Several people looked at them surprised as they passed by.

Out at Mads Nedergård's property, Tacit walked down a field boundary with the two others behind him. The footing was a bit rough, but eventually they made it up onto the hill from where they could look down on all sides.

A bit to the one side there was a large stone surrounded by grass and weeds. Tacit had always imagined that it once had sat on the hilltop. It seemed like that would have been more fitting. He led the two men over to it and around to the opposite side where a fox apparently had tried to make an entrance. A hole, deep as an arm, led beneath the stone, and the removed earth fanned out from it down the hillside. It seemed to have been stirred up.

Nielsen-Snook bent over the hole.

"Not much to find here," he mumbled, looking a bit disappointed over the spread-out dirt.

Neither Tacit nor Melin said anything.

Nielsen-Snook took off his jacket and knelt beside the hole.

"It gave up," he said.

"There are three other foxholes in the hill," Tacit told him.

"With foxes in them?"

"I haven't checked."

Teacher Melin walked around the hill and knelt down next

to each foxhole in turn, sniffing at each entrance.

"One of them definitely smells occupied," he reported back.

Nielsen-Snook grumbled unceremoniously and began working at the fourth hole where he found the ragged piece of hide partly buried in the excavated dirt. He laid it carefully in his case.

Tacit sat down on a smaller stone nearby and watched as the stranger scraped loose dirt out of the hole with a trowel. Then Nielsen-Snook stuck his arm in. The position was awkward, and Tacit had to admit that at least the man didn't just give up. After groping around a little, with a triumphant shout he pulled out his hand and opened it, revealing a coin on his palm.

"I thought I had heard something. I hit it with the shovel. It was on edge in the firm ground at the bottom of the hole. We are on the right track."

Tacit decided not to remind him about the one hundred and twenty-six other coins. Melin was also conspicuously quiet.

"There are probably more," said Nielsen-Snook.

Melin came over, appearing interested, while the other scraped around in the foxhole with the trowel.

Suddenly another coin appeared, this time high up on the side wall of the hole. And then shortly after, one more coin.

His excitement kept Nielsen-Snook at his awkward labors for a very long time. He sifted all through the dirt outside the hole as well, but no more silver turned up.

That whole stone should be moved away," he said finally, drying his forehead with his rather dirty sleeve.

Neither Melin nor Tacit felt compelled to take up the hidden directive.

"Would that be appropriate?" asked Melin carefully.

"Appropriate, propriate—we're talking about an invaluable silver treasure. Not to mention our reputation."

"Exactly," agreed Melin. "We don't want to make a bad name for ourselves. I mean, that stone has been sitting there since…

since….”

“Yes, since the grave was robbed,” said Nielsen-Snook dryly.

Tacit stood up.

“May Mortensen go now?” he asked politely.

“Yes, yes.” Nielsen-Snook sounded like he had forgotten the blacksmith’s apprentice was still there.

That same evening, Tacit walked out to the Water Farm and met Ælgar, who stopped and stared at him menacingly.

“What is it I’m hearing?” the old man began.

“Should I know?”

“Who is going to come here?”

“Is someone coming?”

“And dig up the floor in the house?”

“Who said that?”

“Then it’s true?”

“I’m going to dig in the great room. I’m going to tear up the floor tonight.”

Ælgar glared belligerently at the crowbar in Tacit’s hand.

“Nothing is going to be torn up,” he said angrily.

“It’s rotten all through it. I might as well remove it. We can burn it.”

“You can’t burn a floor that isn’t yours.”

Tacit felt stuck. He thought that he would take out the whole floor so no one could see that it was all broken in front of the stove. It was dumb of Malvina to tell Ælgar about their conversation, he thought. Ælgar always bristled at any changes on the farm.

“I thought maybe I could put a new floor in there,” he said, trying again.

“You can’t put down floors in other people’s houses,” said Ælgar.

Tacit looked at the old man.

Then he said, “I’m thinking about buying the Water Farm.”

Ælgar caught his breath.

"You?" He snorted like a horse. "And what do you have to buy it with?"

"Nothing yet," admitted Tacit.

Strange that Malvina didn't tell him about the coins under the floor, he thought.

"There you see. Just leave that floor alone until you've got something. We don't want anyone coming out here. You got that?"

They walked together in silence around to the kitchen door, where Tacit leaned his crowbar against the wall. Inside the kitchen, Malvina looked at him with worried eyes, and little Mina sat curled up in the back corner of the bed, seemingly afraid.

At the sight of Tacit she pushed herself away from the bed and walked in as big an arc as the room allowed over to Ælgar, where she sought refuge by cleaving to him.

"What's wrong?" asked Tacit, confused. He looked at Malvina, but Malvina's eyes were riveted to the three-year-old.

No one answered him for a long time.

"Do you want to say it yourself? Or should I do it?" asked Malvina, without removing her gaze from Mina.

The little girl raised her face a bit from Ælgar's coarse coat and looked at Malvina with one eye.

"You do it," she whispered.

"Please tell me what's going on," asked Tacit again. "Did she do something wrong?"

"She's the one who told," said Malvina solemnly. "And she knows she shouldn't have."

"That someone was going to come dig in the floor?" asked Tacit

Malvina nodded, and Ælgar picked up Mina onto his lap.

"Meen is a good girl," he said, cuddling her.

Tacit looked from one to the other.

Then, without conviction, and to no one in particular, he said "Well, I guess I might as well tell the whole story."

Malvina nodded again.

"I figured she was right, the little one," mumbled Ælgar. "Meen doesn't just make up things like that."

Tacit sat quietly for a moment. The others waited. And then he began telling again how he had stepped through the floor in the great room, how the end of the board had come up when he removed his foot, and how he couldn't help but see that there were some coins lying in the dirt underneath.

"You could have just not gone in there in the first place," mumbled Ælgar reproachfully. "Why would you go in there anyway?"

Tacit didn't answer him, but kept telling about what he found, about how shaken up he was when he saw how many coins there were and how old they were, and, not least of all, how much they weighed when he put them in his pockets.

"You could have just left them there," snarled Ælgar.

While Tacit talked, Malvina went around straightening up the kitchen, putting things away and taking out the large clay dish. Tacit didn't pay it any mind; he was too preoccupied with his own adventures. When she poured flour in the dish, then milk, and stirred it, then added salt and egg and stirred it again, it still didn't attract his attention.

He still didn't notice, even when all the others started paying attention to her. It wasn't until she took out the butter crock and put a clump of butter on the pan that Tacit thought it was a bit unusual. But he kept talking. He wanted them to hear how shaken up he had been, and how he had finally gone over to see Teacher Melin to find out what he should do.

Ælgar sat staring into space as if none of this had anything to do with him, though it was evident to Tacit that he was still listening. Ælgar did not miss a word, and occasionally he gave a defiant grunt.

The only thing Tacit didn't tell them about were the small figurines he had sold. He didn't want anything to diminish his tale.

"Why couldn't you just have left them there where they were?" asked Ælgar. "It wasn't your money. It was none of your business."

"Who should have found them instead?" Tacit asked.

"No one. They were fine where they were."

Malvina spooned a ladleful of batter onto the pan and spread it out. It steamed marvelously and Ælgar lifted his head and breathed it in.

Then Tacit said, "They say I'll get a finder's fee."

"Who's they?"

"Melin and the man they sent."

"You have sold us out," said Ælgar bitterly. "That's what you've done."

Tacit denied it.

"Then what have you done?" the old man asked.

"I told Melin to see if he could get me a price on the Water Farm."

Ælgar stared at Tacit astounded.

"You—you–," he stammered. "Have you gone completely crazy?"

Malvina stood straight up. She turned her head and just looked at Tacit.

"For a finder's fee?" shouted the old man, grabbing his head. His face expressed such dismay that Tacit was suddenly gripped by doubt.

"I should be able to save up for the difference," he said unconvincingly. "Soon I'll be earning a worker's pay."

"Then you're dumber than I ever imagined. What a hole. You can't spend money on this. There's nothing here that's good for anything. The buildings are crumbling and the land is useless." The old man sat there.

Then he said, "And what about me?" with something that resembled despair. "And what about Ingelin?"

"What do you mean?"

"If you really do buy this place and tear it down and build it up and make it livable, where am I going to live?"

"Here, of course. The Water Farm is nothing without you." Tacit felt offended that the old man thought he would just be thrown out. "You and Ingelin both will stay here, of course," he said.

"Nonsense. I know all this is just for you and her there." Ælgar snickered and tossed his head in the direction of Malvina, who blushed and looked away so they wouldn't see it. But Tacit noticed.

"Now you're the one who's being dumb," said Tacit. "You were here first. You and Ingelin."

"Sure. I know what I know," mumbled Ælgar.

"Just wait and see," said Tacit. "We're all going to live here." Ælgar shook his head.

"It will never work," he muttered with a surly skepticism. "It'll never happen."

"Well, it's working right now," said Tacit.

"That's only because none of us are allowed to be here—and because it's been so long since anyone was. As soon as someone stirs things up –."

"Then what?"

"People will start paying attention. You should have left the silver there."

"They think I found them under a boulder on Eagle Hill," said Tacit.

"You asked about a price—that's all it takes. Do you think the owner will sell the place without coming to look at it first? Then everything will come out—how I've been living here illegally for years—and that Meen is here. They'll find out everything—about her, too." He pointed at Malvina. "She's not old enough to have a child. She'll be put in an orphanage. Meen will be too. And me—what do you think they'll do with me— I'll end up in an institution." Ælgar's voice was bitter.

They stared at him in horror. And for the first time Tacit thought that it probably would have been a good idea to just leave the coins where they were. The prospects that Ælgar painted for them were so dark it was hard to bear.

"No!" exclaimed Tacit. "No."

Then Malvina turned her back to the stove. While the others had been talking, she had been making thin pancakes. She had placed them one by one on Ælgar's cutting board, and now she stood there holding it. Her face was unmistakably pale, and her lips were closed so tightly her mouth was just a fine line, but her eyes were open wide and full of something that Tacit couldn't quite discern.

"I figured it was too good to last," she said. "But if what Ælgar says is true, then it's time for you to learn what kind of person you have taken in." She set the tray down on the table and gave out plates as usual. Then she got the crock with the fine sugar.

"Help yourselves," she said.

Malvina's Story

"**T**here you go. Take some."

Obediently, they each took a little mound of sugar on their plates and rolled up a pancake to dip into it.

After Malvina, for a long while, just sat looking down into her lap, Tacit asked gingerly, "Is it about the woman who wanted you to stay?"

She shook her head.

"There's not so much to tell about her," she said. "And I don't know if it's a good idea to tell it backwards. It's probably best if I begin with my mother, back home, because ever since I was little she told me that I should keep away from men. She didn't want what happened to her to happen to me.

"At first I didn't know what she meant. But since she never missed a chance to warn me, by telling me about girls who had gotten into trouble and were going to have babies, and how they always ended up miserable, eventually I began to understand that the baby was the trouble and that it was the man's fault.

"She told me about how no one would hire a girl like that, because then they would have to feed the child too, and how that kind of girl would have go around begging and, in the end, end up at the poorhouse.

"Or even worse, how they went to jail, if they tried to escape their shame by taking the baby's life. She told me the luckiest ones were probably the ones who put themselves in the bog while they still could. But then they lost their chance at salvation. They didn't bother anyone during the day, but you could chance meeting them at night because their souls were not at peace."

Tacit could see how Malvina shivered at the thought of it, but also how she was determined to continue with her story.

"There was no way out for girls who got into trouble," she continued, "except to find themselves some miserable fellow who was willing to marry her because no one else would have him. That was what happened to my mother. She just barely made it to the altar with him before I was born.

"But then there's no chance of ever being respectable again, and your life is never going to be normal." Malvina poked distractedly at the sugar with the end of her pancake, but didn't eat any.

"But he always treated me good," she continued softly. "They called him Magpie because he was always collecting things. Still I have more respect for him than for the man who deserted my mother after she got pregnant."

There was something like spite in Malvina's voice, and Tacit noticed that she held her head more erect.

"I was determined not to get into trouble," she said. "But even though I did as my mother said and kept my distance from all the farmhands, and got a job on a farm where there were no sons, I couldn't escape.

"I slept in a little room in the attic gable over the scullery, and one night I woke up because someone was touching me. The mistress didn't have any other girls. I was alone in the room, and I tried to make myself disappear into the bed, as if I weren't there.

"A hand crept over the bedclothes, and there was someone next to me breathing heavily. I was so scared my chest hurt. The hand could tell I was there and it pulled on the blanket, and I couldn't even scream, not really anyway. Not much sound came out.

"'Be quiet,' a voice said. It was Master. It was his hand pulling on the covers.

"So I screamed and tried to cover myself, but his hand just moved over my mouth, smothering the sound.

"'Be quiet, girl,' he hissed.

"With his other hand he lifted the covers off of me and started to pull up my shift. I fought him and twisted and tried to kick him away, but he was much too strong and much too heavy. He just turned over on top of me.

"'Just lie there,' he demanded, 'there's no point yelling.'

"I was screaming into his hand, but it just sounded like a distant sob and was no use. So I bit him. I bored my teeth into that hand he was holding over my mouth and clamped down on the flesh and sawed and sawed with no other thought than getting away.

"Master cursed angrily, but he didn't move his hand. He just squeezed my nostrils together until I passed out. He was gone when I came to.

"I cried and felt scared and didn't know what I should do, and in the morning there was blood on the bed and on my shift. When I came downstairs, Master was standing there getting bandaged by Mistress, and next to them was a cloth he had wound around his hand while he was sleeping. There was a lot of blood on it. She was scolding him for not saying anything when he came in, and then he said that he didn't want to wake her just because the sow bit him. He had been sitting over in the barn with a sow that was going to farrow before he crept up the ladder to my room. Mistress was mad because a sow bite gets infected easily, and I didn't dare look at either of them, but I took the ash pan from the stove and went outside."

Malvina stopped, staring straight ahead. "It seems like so long ago, more than a year, but still it feels like it just happened.

"From then on he often came up the ladder," she said, sighing. "Every time a cow was sick or was going to calve or every time a sow was going to farrow." She looked down-hearted.

"Couldn't you have locked the door?" asked Tacit quietly.

Malvina shook her head.

"It didn't lock. There was no hasp or hook or anything."

"But couldn't you block it with something? A cabinet or a

dresser?"

"There wasn't any cabinet or dresser in the room, and besides it opened outwards." She sat for a while with her gaze turned inward, reviewing all the speculations she had made to try to escape.

Then she said, "I tried to hide under the bed, but he found me right away and pulled me out. There were no other places to hide, and I had to sleep in the room I was given. And when I tried to resist he forced me and threatened to strangle me if I yelled."

"Why didn't you say something to Mistress?"

"I didn't dare. She would just have thrown me out, and I would have had a bad reputation after my first job. And I didn't want to disappoint my mother."

It hurt Tacit to look at her. What was happening inside her mind was evident outwardly in her eyes. Also Ælgar was affected by her story. His jaw was clenched as were his hands. Malvina's hand was still holding the first pancake. She breathed deeply before continuing.

"Some time later I started to throw up," she said. "Every morning it happened, when Mistress stood in the scullery below, yelling through the ladder access hole that it was daytime and time to get up. I didn't need to see her to know how she looked with her wrinkled shift and unkempt hair, big and heavy and sleepy, with her feet in a pair of worn-out, crocheted wool slippers.

"As soon as she was gone I pulled over the night pail and vomited into it. It tasted sour and strong, and at first I hoped it would pass, that it was from something I had eaten, since I often was given food that was half-moldy, which Mistress thought was still good enough for me. But it wasn't long before I realized what it was.

"It was trouble.

"It was my own ruin.

"It was exactly what my mother had warned me against. What must not happen. That was what dumped out into the bucket every morning as soon as I sat up.

"And every day I felt the fear in my belly, the fear of being found out, which burned and tugged and made it so I could hardly eat. At the table I felt Mistress's eyes probing me as I sat, poking at my food. Her hard, piercing stare would not leave me alone.

"'You're not eating,' she announced. 'Are you sick?'"

"I shook my head and turned my face towards my plate.

"'If you're not sick, then what is it?' she wanted to know.

"'It's nothing,' I lied.

"'Is the food not good enough for you, the way you're sitting there poking at it?'

"I felt caught and had to force myself to swallow a couple more bites. At the same time I realized that there was no way to escape the misery awaiting me.

"But it still wasn't visible. I was just as small and scrawny as when I had been hired in March, just as thin and ashen and sallow.

"'Eat,'" demanded mistress. "'I think I'm doing a good deed by hiring a poor man's daughter like you, and then you sit there turning down my food.'"

"I had to pinch myself hard in my leg to keep from crying. I knew very well that she hadn't hired me to help me in any way. It was only because she could hire me cheaply, and because I was a hard worker. She hired me because she could pay me next to nothing. Just lodging and a pair of clogs at Christmas.

"And the food I got wasn't much different from what they fed the farm dog. It was the same with Arvid, he was also the child of a poor man and he sat across from me at the table. The plate of meatballs never made it to where we sat, and the tray of sausages never came to us at dinner, either. But Arvid was older. And he wasn't pregnant. At the end of the table sat

Master, shoveling in his food. There was never anything wrong with his appetite.

"Once in a while I felt so furious because he just sat there pretending, as if he didn't know what was happening. But I had to bottle up my anger, because there was no other recourse. I had to admit that it was true what my mother had said in her bitter voice. That it is always the girl who suffers. I was absolutely sure I was going to be chased out the door as soon as Mistress could see how things were. I would get the blame and the shame, and Master would go free.

"As the summer progressed, every day I expected that Mistress would corner me and question me. But it didn't happen until the berry harvest, while we each stood in front of a bush.

"'Now you had better come out and tell it like it is,' she began. And I knew immediately what she meant.

"Now, I thought: *here we go.*

"My thoughts were spinning around and around. What could I say? I couldn't deny it because she could tell. So I didn't answer."

"'Answer me!'

"Mistress stabbed her voice into me as if it were a knife. But I still didn't know what I should say. I had to think about my mother. She would condemn me, because she had warned...

"'Who is the father of the kid?' Mistress cut in, since I was still silent.

"I turned my head away. I felt dizzy and I had to hold onto the bush to keep from falling. This was the moment my world would collapse. There would be nothing left. I could already feel that I was dying."

Tacit looked from Malvina to Ælgar's hands opening and closing at the edge of the table.

"Mistress came and grabbed me by the shoulders and shook me," continued Malvina.

"'Don't just stand there making a fuss,' she demanded. 'Get

yourself together and answer my question!'

"I could feel how unsteady I was on my feet."

"'You can just as well tell me now,' she continued. 'Who is the father of your child?'

"*Your*, I thought. Already the baby was mine. My mother was right.

"Deep inside my body, all the way in where the baby was, I felt an anger growing. A hate for both Mistress and Master. It gushed through me and sent a warmth through my body, all the way out to my freezing cold hands and feet. And for the first time I looked directly at Mistress. How she stood there with her solid legs and her wide hips and strong arms. She was just as strong as Master, I could never overpower her. But her anger would reach him.

"'Well?' she said.

"I held onto the bush so tight my knuckles were white. It was the turning point.

"'Master did it,' I heard myself say.

"My hatred slung the words at her body as if they had been stones, and I stared at her and kept staring at her, knowing that this was my ruin, for eternity. There would be no way back. Now my world would collapse.

"But at the same time I felt the hate like an unbending, hard object, up through my body inside my spine, something that made me stand erect and kept me upright.

"Mistress's face went white, but only for a brief, shocking instant, then her red blood streamed back in and her eyes flashed like lightning. A cracking blow made me fall back into the bush and down.

"'You're lying!'

"Mistress stood towering over me.

"'He came up the ladder at night!' I screamed as loud as I could.

"'You're lying!'

"'He's the one who did it! He raped me!'

"And Mistress knew it was true, but she couldn't accept it. Her eyes were wild, she could have killed me. But I couldn't stop. The words poured out of me like a torrent.

"'It was me that bit him in the hand!' I screamed. 'It wasn't the sow!'

"'You bitch…you hussy…you…you…'

"Then she checked herself and her eyes narrowed.

"'Don't think you're going to get away with this,' she hissed. 'You will never have anything over Master. It's Arvid that did this to you. You know that as well as I.'

"One of her strong arms reached down into the bush and pulled me up.

"'So come out and admit it,' she demanded, shaking me.

"'No!' I yelled.

"A whack on the other side of my head made me fall again.

"'Tell the truth!' she demanded.

"'There was never anyone but Master!' I yelled, hysterical.

"'How dare you smear Master's name.'

"Mistress looked for something to hit me with. I think she wanted to force me to admit it was Arvid. But I felt that rigid strength in my back. I wouldn't. I wouldn't. But she had the upper hand.

"'Then ask him yourself,' I screamed wildly. 'Ask him where he went at night after being in the barn!' Again the words streamed from my mouth before I even realized it. I heard my voice screaming in her face, that he had held my mouth, nearly suffocating me, that there was blood everywhere afterwards, and that I had bit him trying to get free.

"'You damned tramp!' yelled Mistress back at me. And having nothing else to hit me with, she started kicking me in the legs with her clogs, while I scampered farther and farther back into the ruined bush. When she couldn't kick me any more, she stood there breathing like a bellows.

"She panted, 'Say it! It was Arvid, wasn't it?'

"'No!' I answered defiantly, fully expecting she was going to beat me to death.

"But instead, she screamed, 'Pack up your belongings and get out! Right now! I never want to see you again as long as I live!'

"I crawled out of the bush on the opposite side and, dazed, I got to my feet. Mistress pointed to the house with an outstretched arm and I saw her hand shaking. Half-senselessly I stumbled in that direction, around the house and in through the scullery, up the rungs to my room. Everything was a blur, and I was making sounds I didn't recognize, a moaning, a quiet hollow mumbling without meaning.

"My church skirt, and the nice top that wasn't as nice as it once was. The woolen winter shawl that I had gotten from my grandmom when she died, and the comb that also had been hers, big and coarse, made of yellowed bone. My things didn't take up much room, and I bundled them all up in my headscarf, put my old worn-out clogs from last winter on my feet, and hurried down the ladder again, terrified that Mistress would come after me before I got away.

"Outside the scullery door my legs started to run all on their own. Away, just away, to find some place I could hide. But not out on the town road where people could see me. The disgrace of being thrown out from a farm was so unbearable that my feet led me instead through the dungheap, behind the barn, and out on the farm road, and on and on, trailing only the quiet howling that forced its way out through my teeth. It wasn't crying; it was the sound of death. My life was over, I knew this. Inside my head I heard only my mother's voice.

"*While you still can*, it said. *While you still can.*

"And I still could. There was only one way to avoid disgracing my parents. My body knew where it needed to go and it found its way along windbreaks and the edges of woods. And my feet did not stop running when my eyes saw the water glinting in the peaceful peat pits.

"Don't stop now. Don't think, don't think."

Malvina stopped talking.

They all sat staring at her, stiff and unmoving. The only one who had touched her pancakes was little Mina. Even though most of Malvina's story had gone over her head, she clearly absorbed the concentrated, almost petrified anticipation of the two men. It was translated by her into unease and nervousness, and she had unconsciously attempted to alleviate her fears by stuffing herself.

She had gobbled down both her own and Ælgar's pancakes, and they were large. In the stillness that hung over the kitchen, she wormed her way down onto the floor and wandered directly over to the bed, where she climbed up next to Comfort, who was lying there playing with her own fingers. Then she immediately fell asleep.

"But eat, eat," Malvina burst out saying at the sight of so many pancakes still left, piled up on the cutting board. "They're getting cold."

She passed a new one over onto Ælgar's plate, but he just sat there as if he didn't even notice. Tacit didn't move either.

"Why don't *you* eat?" said Tacit in retaliation, when she looked at the half-pancake still left on his plate. She still had a whole one on hers.

No one spoke while they ate. They were preoccupied with images from Malvina's story. And now that they were eating, they took seconds, too, so she wouldn't feel that she had done all that work for nothing.

"What happened then?" asked Tacit, wiping up the last of his sugar with a stump of pancake.

Malvina silently shook her head.

"It's late," she said. Then she walked over and took Comfort from the arms of Mina, who was sleeping soundly. She brought her back to the table and started inserting little pieces of pancake into her mouth.

"But you can't stop now," said Tacit.

"It's much too late," said Malvina.

Tacit insisted. "You have to tell us the rest. We're not going to be able to sleep now, anyway." He turned, appealing to Ælgar, who just nodded.

Instead of answering, Malvina asked, "Can you pass me the milk?"

Tacit reached his arm back and got hold of the milk jug and Mina's cup that was standing on the windowsill.

After she had given Comfort a drink, he asked, "What did you do then?"

"I shut my eyes," she said.

"You shut your eyes?" Tacit sounded appalled and Ælgar shifted position against the stiff backrest.

"My feet kept running. There was only one way out. Just something to be over and done with."

"You mean you kept going out into the peat pits?"

"Yes."

"Didn't you think about going home to your mother?"

"That's the one thing I couldn't do," said Malvina, putting another piece of pancake into the baby's mouth. "When I felt myself fall it was almost like a relief. It was done and couldn't be undone. I dove in sort of sideways and I saw the smooth surface break apart.

"Then I reached out like you do when you fall, but there was only water there. The deep, brackish, icy cold closed around me, got under my clothes and against my skin. It struck me that this was how it was. I had thought that I would just disappear, sink down like I was sleeping and then everything would be over. I screamed with terror and my mouth filled with water.

"Beneath me my legs were running and running to touch something solid, and my hands slapped the surface for something to grab. And the whole time I felt something pulling me down, something grabbing me, panicking me with fear.

"I got my head up over the surface and breathed and realized that I was very close to the edge, but there was no foothold. The peat pit was dug straight down, and the soft muddy wall gave way when I touched it. Then I went under again.

"My feet kept running and my arms churned the surface until my head made it up again and I could breathe. Then I reached my arm towards the rim and caught a thin root sticking out just over the water. Carefully I pulled myself closer while my legs kept churning, and when the root broke off I grabbed a clump of grass. My hand pounced on it like a bird of prey, and the fingers of my other hand bored into the peat next to it, and I hung there catching my breath. I breathed and breathed and had only one thing in my mind—getting out.

"But as soon as my legs dangled down in the depths, I could feel the icy cold grabbing for me to take me down. There was no bottom.

"But I wouldn't, I wouldn't go down there. My heart was hammering in my chest, and with a big breath I pulled myself up so I was able to grab a farther clump of grass with my one hand. My fear spurred me on. My wet clothes clung to my body, weighing me down, but I had to, I needed to, and I kicked with my legs so nothing from below could get them.

"Then I curled myself up and dug my toes deep into the peaty ground as high up as I could, and hand over hand I pulled myself up onto my belly so only my legs were dangling in the water. I lay there totally exhausted for a long while. I could just barely sense the sun warming me and how the earth and grass held me up. My head was totally devoid of thoughts and my eyelids closed out the world, as if I had died, like I had fallen asleep. High above there were larks singing and I don't know how long I lay there like that.

"That was when I felt it.

"I was lying totally still, but suddenly awake and with all my attention directed inward. There was something moving—inside me—like a mouse.

"I thought that maybe I had died after all. Or that something from the peat pit had gotten inside me. A frog? A fish? Then the movement came again.

"The baby?

"My baby. It was moving, it was alive. I wasn't alone in my body anymore. I had tried to drown myself; the baby was trying to comfort me. The thought was so overwhelming that I started to cry.

"Then I realized my feet were still in the water, and I pulled myself up and turned over on my back with my arms folded over my belly. I had never thought about it before as a living thing, something that would die if I killed myself. I had only felt it as a problem, the visible evidence of my disgrace.

"And I had hated that baby from the moment I had started vomiting and I had only thought of it as a part of Master that had stayed inside me. And I lay there, dripping wet, nearly drowned, and starting to feel tenderness for it. How could that be?

"Neither Master nor Mistress would have anything to do with it. They chased it away when they chased me from the farm. And I couldn't bring it home to my own mother—there was no one who would take care of it but me. I had never wanted a baby but I had one anyway and it was mine alone.

"While I lay there thinking, the anger came back. Not anger towards the baby, but anger that I should be judged for something that was not my fault. It was Master who had acted wrongly. Why should that cost my life? An ordinary life.

"The whole town would judge me as a depraved female. And Mistress would definitely make it look like it was Arvid who had climbed the ladder. No one would believe him if he said that it wasn't him, because who else could it be? But no one would expect him to go drown himself.

"The anger triggered inside me a resistance and a desire to stretch. And so I lay there in the grass stretching, and then I sat up and looked around at where I was—right at the edge of the peat pit, with all my misery intact.

"So I wasn't meant to die. Otherwise the water would have kept me. I was meant to live with this baby I had inside me. I just didn't know how.

"Then I noticed my bundle that I had been carrying in my hand. It was perched on a mound of sedges right on the rim, where it landed when I fell in. It was like a gift.

"My clogs were floating far out on the surface.

"The sight of them filled me with horror, because it looked like I was dead on the bottom, and the fear I had felt when I was in the water returned to me for a moment. It was that fear which had woken the baby, had gotten it to move, I was sure of it. And when I looked at the floating clogs I could picture myself lying in the brown, muddy, dark depths down at the bottom.

"It would also look like that to others who came by, I thought. They would definitely think I had drowned.

"The thought was new and strange and I couldn't get it out of my mind. So I was dead anyway, even though I made it out of the peat pit. It was strange. But as long as they didn't know, they couldn't do anything to hurt me.

"It almost felt like a liberation. I could move to another part of the country and take on a new name, and no one would know who I was or what had happened to me. My bad reputation would remain here where I had lived before.

"Carefully I neared the edge of the water and picked up my bundle. It was all I owned and everything in it had been handed down to me from others. The church clothes were from when my mother was a young girl, and they had belonged to her mother before her. So I turned away from where I grew up and became someone who lived on the road. I would beg for meals, sleep in barns and outbuildings, and let things happen, however they would. I was dead and I didn't belong anywhere any more.

"But it was heavy to walk with the wet skirt slapping against my legs. And anyway how could I go anywhere in daylight. Someone would see me. I had to wait until nightfall.

"That was when I saw the hay barn. It was close by, just past where the ground was higher. I could stay in there while my clothes dried. I had helped fill that barn myself, with good hay, in the middle of the summer. So it didn't seem like too much to ask for it to shelter me until I was ready to go.

"The door creaked when I opened it a bit, squeezed in, and closed it behind me. The only light inside was what slipped through the cracks and gaps, but after a bit I could see well enough not to collide with the hay racks standing against the inside of the gable. I crawled on all fours up onto the huge mountain of hay that had sunk just enough so I could climb across it all the way to the back wall. Here I took off my wet clothing and spread it out. Then I dug my way down inside the pile. And I fell asleep."

The Apparition

There was dead silence in the kitchen. Both Ælgar and Tacit were waiting for Malvina to resume her story; she couldn't just stop there. But Malvina didn't continue.

Ælgar cleared his throat, waiting. Tacit bit his tongue so he wouldn't ask her. Malvina just sat there, staring into the distance. Silence hung over them.

Eventually, without looking at either of them, she said, "It has been a long evening."

No one answered.

"It's been night for quite a while," she continued.

"Morning is still a long ways off," said Tacit.

"Don't you have to go home?"

"Not before I've heard the rest of it."

"I'm too tired."

"You can sleep tomorrow," said Ælgar. "I'll take the children."

Tacit held his breath while Malvina's and Ælgar's eyes met. It was the first thing the old man had said since Malvina had begun her story. She felt that it meant something to him that she told the whole thing. So she got up and put her baby back in bed with Mina.

"When I awoke it was the middle of the night," she began.

They nodded.

"I was very hungry. I reached out and felt my skirt, but it was still too wet. I couldn't go anywhere in that. I felt my underclothes; they were almost dry, so I took them and slipped them on. Then I lay quietly in my cave of hay, waiting.

"Hunger was gnawing at me, and the vision of Mistress's garden floated before my closed eyes. The whole summer I had weeded those beds and I knew exactly what was ripe. If I ran over, dressed as I was, I could get something fast.

"Still I hesitated. Margareta Skadde's daughter had never stolen anything.

"But Margareta Skadde's daughter was dead. Now I was to begin my new life, taking care of myself and doing whatever I had to, even though I had never done it before.

"And besides that, Mistress owed me. I was supposed to have gotten new clogs at Christmas. That gave me more resolve. I felt for my damp work apron, and with that in my hand, I slid down from the hay and snuck out into the wet grass.

"The peat pits were steaming and the air was damp and raw, even though it was still summer. It was easy to run with so little clothes on. By the garden I stopped and listened, but everything was quiet. No one was waking up yet. So I went in and spread out my apron next to the carrot bed. I felt with my fingers for the thickest roots and laid them on my apron with the tops still on. I didn't want to twist them off there, but I did take the time to cover the holes of those I pulled out.

"After I had collected a big pile in my apron, I went over to the peas and quickly picked as many as I could. I dropped the cold pods down inside my shift until they protruded like a fat bulge over the waistband of my pants. Then I tied up the apron and hurried back.

"At the edge of the bog I broke off all the carrot tops and stuffed them far back under a dense bush. Then I dumped the roots down into a water-filled ditch and rinsed off the apron. I rubbed most of the dirt off of the carrots and laid them back in the damp apron. They didn't take up as much room and now they were ready to eat.

"Up in the hay I wriggled down into my cave again. As soon as I filled my belly I fell asleep.

"I woke up hearing lots of voices, and I sat up terrified. The voices had woken me. Some of them were close by and some farther away. It must have been near noon because the sun was baking the shingle roof, warming below, where I was sitting.

Even my thick skirt was dry.

"Carefully I crept to the back wall where a knot had fallen out. I was startled to see men and farm boys from the village walking along the closest peat pit, holding long poles and fire hooks.

"They were looking for me.

"I was so scared it felt like my heart was going to jump out of my throat. My first impulse was to dash out the meadow door and away from the place. But I held myself back. Even though that door faced away from the peat pits, they would notice me—and then what?

"Wouldn't the whole village feel ridiculous? And then wouldn't they take it out on me? I crept back down into the hay and waited.

"They walked around poking down into the peat pit with their poles. I could feel it in my bones that they were trying to fish me out, and I shivered despite the heat from the roof. They walked around, probing for my dead body. But the poles could only reach near the bank, and the fire hooks looked much too short. If I hadn't been so scared I would have cried for the poor girl lying down there.

"Of course I knew all of them, and I could feel their uneasiness. Everyone wanted to bring me up, but no one wanted to be the one to find me. The strangest part was that I was more aware of the ones who weren't there—first and foremost, Master—he wasn't there.

"I felt a bit of satisfaction inside, that maybe he felt guilty and knew it all was his fault, even though he would never ever admit it to anyone else.

"Arvid was there. Thin and lanky, he stood there helplessly with his pole and couldn't bring himself to stick it in the water. He had probably been sent in Master's place.

"My mother wasn't there, and I was glad for that. The sight of her would have been too much to bear when I was so close.

"But Magpie was there. He didn't have a pole or a hook. He just watched while the others walked around poking the water, and the way he stood seem accusatory. He blamed them. They looked askance at him and kept their distance.

"A little ways from the men, the women grouped together. There were quite a few of them and they were there to see me pulled out. They would stare at my belly through my wet clothing and they would shiver with burning indignation.

"There was a buzz among the women. They put their heads close together and their gaze followed Arvid. They turned towards him and felt their scorn justified. Meanwhile he stood stooped over, his head hanging, not knowing what to do with himself. Mistress had laid the blame on him, and he knew if he protested that he would be fired on the spot.

"In the center of the women stood Mistress, guiding their assumptions. To her I was a wretched offspring of unfortunates and doomed beforehand. —Wasn't this what happened to my mother? This was just what anyone would have expected.

"I was boiling with anger inside, while I sat there with my eye at the knothole. And I regretted that I hadn't told anyone who would listen what Master had done to me, back when it first started.

"Then I felt the baby inside me moving, and I laid my hands on my belly to comfort it. I vowed that Master would never get the chance to even see the child.

"Down at the peat pit the men walked back and forth along the rim. Some walked around the other sides, the women following them hesitantly as a group. The women kept their distance. They never got close to the men, but they were eager to see me brought up to the surface so they could gather me up and put me in the ground. It would be more comfortable for them knowing I was buried—even if it was outside the church cemetery stone wall.

"It lasted a long while. Then they finally gave up. The women remembered everything they had left behind—what they had been in the middle of doing when the news came, and they had abruptly left. Now suddenly they saw in their minds the dough that had been placed to rise, how it was swelling over the rim of the bowl and dumping down onto the table top. Or they remembered the children who had been left alone.

"The fever that had smitten their souls—when the news that I had drowned myself leaped from house to house and pulled them outside, down to the peat bog in the middle of the day—now it suddenly subsided, transformed into worry which chased them back home again.

"Finally only the farmhands were left. Then they headed home too, each going their own way with their poles and hooks over their shoulders. One of them tried to pull my clogs to the bank and nearly fell in. Then he walked away too, leaving me in my watery grave. The bog would hold me forever. Everyone had left.

"They felt guilty because they couldn't bring me up, but also relieved, because now it was over. And they hurried, because no one wanted to be the last to leave. No one wanted to be there alone, and no one would willingly go back. The very last to leave was Magpie. And he was the only one who left slowly.

"And there I knelt, high up on top of the hay.

"Unburied.

"But dead. Relegated to tales about how horrible things become when one does things that are taboo, in order to frighten and warn other girls. I sat clenching my teeth at the thought of it. But if they only knew—those hypocritical madams—I felt compelled to get revenge.

"It wouldn't matter that my mother maintained I had always been a well-behaved obedient child; or that it was other people who had brought me this misery.

"Had always been –

"I held the words in my mouth.

"I was not a child any longer—not a well-behaved one nor a child. I was deceased—and I felt deceased. The more I thought about it, the more I felt outside their reach. They couldn't decide over me any longer—no one could. I had the right of the dead to not obey. From now on I would have to do whatever I had to for myself.

"I could stay here and live in the meadow barn.

"The thought swam in and out of me like a fish, gently, questioning. And after having turned itself around several times, it stayed.

"No one had cut peat there in years, and the hay in the barn wouldn't be collected for use until the end of the winter. It was possible. Still I had to think it through several times. I had to be clear that I really was going to act on the privilege of the dead, and at the same time start to live like a wild animal. I would have to drink water from the ditches outside and I would have to eat all my food raw. Would I do that?

"Or would I rather get away quickly from the area and start begging and asking around for a bit of work?

"I thought about the baby.

"If I chose to remain, I would have to stay until the baby was born, and I had no idea when that would be—probably in the middle of the winter.

"If I chose to leave –?

"I lay down and ate some carrots and thought it over again from the beginning. I ate the last peas and slept a little; then I awoke and the thought was still there. In the twilight I snuck outside and drank some water. And when night had fallen I made my way to the village without having yet made up my mind.

"Barefoot and silently, I slipped inside Master's chopping shed, where I knew there was a knife hanging on the wall. He used that knife to cut open sheaves of grain in the winter when he was threshing, and it had hung in its sheath in its place since his father's time—since his grandfather's even. I took it down and tucked it against my chest.

"Then I snuck inside the barn where the empty grain bags hung over a pole so the mice wouldn't build nests inside them. I needed one to put carrots in. I felt around until I found one without holes and patches, and I took it. But my hands felt around some more, and I found more that were in fine shape, and without knowing what I would do with them I took them too, rolled them together and stuck them inside the first one. Something inside me wanted to have them.

"Master's sack needle was stuck in a crack in a post. I knew where it was, and I ran my fingers over the rough wood, found it and placed it inside my apron pocket.

"Then I went out to the garden and filled the sacks with as many carrots and summer apples as I could carry. Then I returned to the meadow barn and went to sleep.

"The entire morning the next day, I kept watch at the knot hole in the wall, but no one came by to poke around in the water with poles and fire hooks. I didn't really expect them to return after how it had gone the day before.

"Next to my sleeping hole lay the rolled-up sacks, and the sight of them filled me with satisfaction. Suddenly I knew why I had taken them. I had built a nest. Without really knowing what I was doing, I had already decided. I was acting like a mouse collecting pieces of wool and moss when it was going to give birth. I was already starting to live like an animal, and just like a mouse or a squirrel, I had to gather food while it was available.

"That is why in many following nights I went around to different gardens in the village, filling my sacks with whatever root vegetables and fruits I found there. Back in the meadow barn I made caches under the hay, filling them with potatoes and cabbages, winter apples and whatever I came across.

"Then came the night when I returned to Mistress's yard

and I saw her laundry hanging between the apple trees. It was shining white under a moonlit sky, where clouds came and went. I stood there rooted to the ground while I thought it over. It was hard to decide.

"*Now is the time to do it.* said the dead one. *Now you must do it for yourself and for your child—if you want to survive.*

"So I dropped the sack under a bush and picked out the largest white piece there—a solid, closely-woven woolen sheet that was big enough for a double bed—big enough to double up and use as a winter coat. It was nearly dry and I stood on the garden path and wrapped it around myself.

"That was when I heard Mistress's clogs tramping across the farmyard towards the garden, and the farm maid inside me wanted to flee, jump over the stone wall and hide. I could have made it. But I felt a devilishness rise inside me. My spine lifted my head erect—I was the dead one—and I flipped an end of the sheet over my head and walked out to meet her. I was standing just barely out of sight, near the house on the gravel garden path, when she turned the corner. I stood completely still.

"The old woman stopped short as if she had been hit by lightning. She stood stock-still, not yet dressed, as if she had just that moment crept out of bed upon remembering her forgotten laundry. She was broad and heavy, her mouth and eyes wide open.

"I looked at her from underneath the flap of the fine woolen sheet and didn't move. For the first time in my life I felt powerful, a sense of being untouchable. And in front of me— Mistress paralyzed with fear. A wild bliss rushed through me at the sight; it felt like I was floating.

"The whole encounter only lasted for a few breaths. Then Mistress's clogs scuttled around in the gravel and she ran screaming back to the door and into the house. I followed the sound of her. In a moment Master would appear with a cane or an axe.

"I used the time to pull down various pieces of clothing from the line—Mistress's long, black wool socks, Master's long, gray underpants, a woolen undershirt plus all the pillowcases that were there. This was my chance, because this would be the last time they hung laundry out at night—both here and in the rest of the village. I was sure of that.

"In one long movement I gathered up the bundle and threw it over the stone wall. Then I grabbed the sack and hopped over. Kneeling on the other side, I stuffed the laundry into the empty, dark brown sack. My own clothes were dark and blended with the surroundings. Even if Master had stuck his head over the stone wall he wouldn't have seen anyone.

"When he eventually appeared around the corner of the house with whimpering and whining Mistress hanging on him, the garden was empty and quiet. All that was left was the remaining laundry, like a row of teeth with some missing. And I still sensed this great floating feeling inside me.

"After that I didn't go into people's gardens much for a long time. In the fields people were starting to harvest grain—and I harvested too. To carry it over my shoulder I had cut a long slit in one of the sacks, and another slit where I could stick the grain spikes in.And every night I walked along the final cuttings of one wheat field, and then another, and I cut the tops with Master's knife.

"Later in the year I collected field beets—not the largest ones—the most manageable ones. It started getting very cold. The nights were wet and windy, and my feet were freezing even though I had packed them in burlap stuffed with hay.

"Still I kept collecting food as long as I could. I didn't know when it would be enough. It wasn't until snow fell and I started leaving a trail that I seriously started to hibernate. But it was colder lying in the straw than I had imagined. Even with Mistress's knitted socks on, and with Master's long underwear over them, and bundled in everything I had, I still was so cold

I was afraid it would make me sick. Icy drafts pressed their way through the leaky wooden walls, cooling the room. It was only in the summer that a place like that could be used for human habitation. If I didn't want to freeze to death when it got really cold, I was going to have to do something.

"Just like the animals did.

"I would have to have shelter from the drafts so I could conserve my body heat. So I dug down deeper—a long hole with steep sides—and inside this cave I stuck pieces of wooden lath from some disassembled hay feeders. And afterwards I covered it over with hay again so it was only a tube I could crawl through—a foxhole with a cave at the bottom. Finally I was warm enough, and down there I slept through the winter."

Malvina stopped talking, pausing for a good while.

"Foxes are good animals," mumbled Ælgar faintly. "They get by."

Tacit turned his head and took at look at Ælgar. Malvina's account had touched something in the old man. There was recognition in his voice and his head nodded up and down, just like Ingelin when there were flies around.

"But you couldn't just sleep the whole time, could you?" he asked, turning his head towards the girl.

"I became a fox," she smiled coyly.

"But sometimes I lay awake too," she admitted, "and I lay there thinking or chewing on wheat kernels or eating a couple of apples. But otherwise I slept. When I had to go out I walked over to the bushes and crouched down, and on the way back I drank wherever water pooled up from the ground. Then I wiped my face with my wet hands or sometimes with snow. Otherwise I lay in my cave and only ate when I was hungry, and days and nights blended together. And the trail of my sack-prints didn't amount to much. The wind and the snow evened them out soon enough. And besides, no one ever came by there."

Malvina paused again, staring straight ahead.

"Not until one day when the barn door creaked open carefully and someone slipped inside. It woke me and my heart was in my throat just like when Master had crept up the ladder.

"I lay there listening, trying to calm the pounding of my heart. And while I listened I stuck my hand down to my chest and pulled the knife out of its sheath—this time he wasn't going to get away with it, I thought—I couldn't imagine that it could be anyone but him.

"It was completely quiet in the barn. Whoever had come inside wasn't moving. No one tried to climb up into the hay. Still I lay there stiff and tense with the knife in my hand.

"Little by little the barn door was opened and closed again, and I heard steps walking away—careful, unhurried steps. When I was sure he had left, I crept down and opened the door a little. There were footsteps of a man in boots. They came from around the corner from the direction of the peat pits, and led away from the door between the hills towards the village.

"Could it be Master?

"I crept up and looked through the knot hole in the back wall. From up there I could see that the footsteps came from the peat pit and that the man had walked along the edge. But I could also tell that he had come from the opposite side from where Master's farm was. Could it be Master? But why would he be walking around here? And if it weren't him, then who was it?

"A couple of days passed and I calmed down. It must have just been a random occurrence. But then on the third day someone was at the door again—it was opened and closed—but no one came inside. And the steps continued on.

"That was strange. I slid down to see who it could be. Just inside the door lay a big clump of cold porridge on a wide shard of pottery.

"I must have stared at it as if it had been a dangerous wild animal.

"Why was it brought there?

"Was it bait?

"And if it was, who were they trying to catch?

"Did the man think animals were living in the hay? Martens or something like that? Marten fur was expensive. Maybe he would return with a trap.

"Or was it me? Had I been discovered?

"I kept staring at the porridge. I hadn't eaten cooked food since Mistress had thrown me out. My mouth was watering. I carefully touched the porridge with my finger—it wasn't even frozen. What harm could it do if I ate it? The man who came in with it couldn't see it was me. The barn wasn't so impenetrable—animals could easily come in at the bottom of the walls where the boards had rotted away in places.

"I stuck my finger in my mouth. It tasted good. I was on the verge of tears and had to taste it again.

"Crouching down and freezing cold, I sat beside the pottery shard and dreamed back to my mother's house. That was the best porridge I had ever had. My saliva-slick fingers continued until there was nothing left, and suddenly I realized what I had done. It was gone. By eating the porridge I might have given myself away—that I hadn't drowned after all.

"A new kind of fear crept into me, and I almost didn't dare to fall asleep again. The rest of the day and most of the night I stayed awake, but then I slept like a bear until the barn door was opened again the next morning.

"I was almost suffocated with fear. Now it was going to happen. He was going to search through the hay and find me. I held my breath until the door was closed again.

"Did he leave?

"Or was it to trick me, to get me to come out? I still took the risk of looking, but all I could see was a dark figure who could have been anyone.

"Then I saw the porridge. This time in a real bowl. And I recognized that bowl. It was the bowl my mother used for yoghurt. I knew every single nick in its chipped edge. It was Magpie.

"He knew I was there and he brought me the porridge. I cried, sitting next to the bowl, gulping down the porridge. And afterwards I cried myself to sleep up in the hay. My bewilderment over finding myself again in a world with other people was so great that I was completely dumbfounded. Just the previous day I had only one path to take, and now it was all changed, or was it?

"When I awoke it was morning and I tried to put on my skirt, but it wouldn't fit around me anymore. I had to tie one of the sack strings around my belly to hold up my apron. Then I ate a carrot and a raw potato, and bundled in my woolen sheet, I sat waiting in front of the knot hole.

"And it really was Magpie who came. But not from the village like I had expected. I could see him approaching from far out in the bog between the many peat pits, and he didn't go straight. He walked here and there as if he were looking for something. I followed him with my gaze until he had nearly reached the barn. Then I sat down in the hay next to the door.

MIDHUSBAND

Malvina stopped talking and sat staring into space. The fire in the stove had long ago gone out. Only the little candle on the table illuminated the room, but the outer edges were all dark. Tacit waited impatiently for Malvina to resume her story while Ælgar just sat there.

She hesitated. Malvina's face revealed an inner reluctance. There was a struggle going on inside her, preventing her from telling more.

Tacit observed her. If she stopped now he would never find out the rest; he was sure of it. But he wanted to know; he wanted to know everything about her, even though some of it was difficult for her to reveal.

He waited as long as he dared.

When the silence had persisted so long that it felt like an enormous blanket, Tacit finally blurted out, "But didn't he go inside?"

"Yes," she answered absently, "he came inside, but he didn't see me right away. Not before I said thank you for the porridge. Then he smiled shyly.

"'I don't have anything for you, today,' he said, apologizing, 'because there was nothing.'

"I felt a slight disappointment, but I knew very well how it was back home when there was nothing to eat. Then I noticed that he wasn't looking at me directly; he kept looking around as if he were kind of afraid.

"'How is Mother?' I asked to help him understand that it really was me sitting there.

"'The way a mother is when her daughter is in trouble,' he answered softly. 'It's been hard on her.'

"'Have you told her that I'm here?' I asked.

"Magpie shook his head. 'Not yet. First I wanted to make sure.'

"'Don't tell her just yet.'

"'Why not? She'll be so happy.'

"'Because—.' I didn't know how to say it. How could I talk about things like that to a man?

"'Just say it,' he said, when he noticed my hesitation.

"I stood up and let the woolen sheet fall down around me.

"'Because of this,' I said.

"Magpie looked shocked at the sight of my changed appearance.

"'But child—,' he blurted out.

"I looked down at myself.

"'So is it true what they said?' he whispered.

"'What did they say?'

"I could hear that my voice was aggressive.

"'That you—that Arvid –'

"Looking at me made Magpie stutter.

"'It wasn't Arvid,' I said abruptly. 'He never did a thing to me.'

"'It's just that they said –'

"Magpie had a confused expression.

"'It was Mistress who said that, wasn't it?' I asked.

"Magpie nodded.

"'But Arvid can't be blamed for what Master did.' I could hear my voice shaking. 'Master did this to me,' I said before he could ask. 'He came up at night and raped me.'

"Magpie turned his face away. I'm sure I looked terrifying, so full of hate.

"'Will it never stop?' he said, setting a heavy sack on the floor. I knew he was thinking of my mother. She had married him out of necessity.

"'Now you know,' I answered quietly.

"'What good is that?'

"'You can tell others.'

"'Who is going to believe someone with a reputation like mine?' He bowed his head dejectedly.

"'I ought to have told them myself—while I still could,' I said. 'But I didn't dare.'

"'Who would have believed you?'

"'It all depends on who you tell—and how,' I said. 'There is always someone who wants to believe the worst about people and spread it around.'

"He nodded pensively. Neither of us spoke for a while.

"Then I asked, 'Did Mistress say that she met me?'

"'Met you?' He looked at me confused. 'What do you mean? Met you where?'

"'In her garden.—Like this.' I flipped the sheet up over my head.

"He laughed.

"'But what will happen when they find out?' he asked, suddenly worried.

"'They won't find out.'

"'What about when you come home?'

"'I'm not coming home.'

"'But you have to. As far as I can see it won't be long before your time.'

"'I'm living like a wild animal,' I said. 'And living like a wild animal I will give birth like a wild animal.' It filled me with a fierce satisfaction to say that.

"'You have changed, little one,' he said softly.

"'Don't tell Mother I'm alive until you know that I'm going to survive,' I answered.

"'But couldn't you still—?' he started to say.

"I shook my head, and he sighed.

"Then he said, 'Your mother has never been so crazy about me. And I understand why. I've never really amounted to much and I've always had a bad reputation. —But when it has gotten so difficult to get enough to eat through honest work....'

"'You have been my father instead of the rotten dog I came from. I'm glad for that,' I said and I meant it. 'From now on I will walk in your footsteps and not in Mother's.'

"'What are you going to do?'

"'The peat pit didn't hold me. If I survive and give birth to my child, it must mean I have a life ahead of me. So I'll leave this place and beg my way.'

"'God have mercy. You be careful,' he muttered sadly.

"'I will,' I said, not really knowing what he meant.

"'Can I come and look in on you while you're here?' he asked.

"I said that was okay.

"'And if I bring some porridge once in a while?' he asked.

"'I will bless you for that,' I said.

"Then I asked what he had in the sack.

"'Bits of peat,' he said. 'I go and kick up the snow everywhere they piled peat during the summer.'

"'But that's far from here,' I said.

"'Yeah,' he said. 'It is far, but while I walk I find some at the old places too.'

"'You can come and look in on me,' I mumbled back to him. 'I'd like that. You are the first person I've talked to since Mistress threw me out.'

"'As often as I can,' he answered solemnly.

"Then I went and dug down deep in the hay with my arms and found a head of cabbage and some carrots for him. Then he left and I went back down in my cave.

"I lay there thinking about what we had said to one another. Something between us had changed, as if we had become more equal. In any case, I had never spoken to him like that before.

"I wondered if it was because for so long he thought I had been dead. Or maybe because I was pregnant now so I wasn't a child any more. He had spoken to me as if I were an adult, and he didn't try to make me go back home.

"After that, Magpie came by regularly. Sometimes he had a bit of porridge with him, other times a couple of cooked potatoes that to me tasted like heaven. In return he got some of what I had left in my stores. A field beet or a couple of onions. Not too much at once. I knew that my mother wouldn't be suspicious if it were only a little bit.

"One day he told me it was Christmas.

"'This is when I would have gotten my clogs,' I said a bit stupidly, and I regretted it even before it had left my mouth.

"He looked down at my feet packed in hay and sackcloth.

"'Do you have frostbite?' he asked.

"I shook my head.

"'Not this year. As long as it's freezing I'm alright,' I said, showing him Mistress's wool stockings. 'It will be worse when thaw comes.'

"Two days later he came by with my old clogs that he had chopped loose from the ice in the peat pit. They were water-logged and pieces of ice and frozen reeds were stuck to them. I received them, gladly surprised.

"'The water wouldn't even keep *them*.' I said.

"'Do they still fit you?' he asked.

"'In my bare feet they do,' I answered, 'but not with straw in them.'

"He wished he could give me a new pair. I could tell by looking at him. But how could he?

"After New Year's, Magpie came by every day. He was worried about me, and I could also feel that the birth was approaching. I thought a lot about the previous two times my mother had given birth. I had been in the kitchen with the neighbor's wife who went back and forth while the midwife was there. She told me what it was I was hearing.

"Then the day came when I couldn't crawl down to meet Magpie and I just wanted him to leave again.

"But he didn't leave. He followed the furrow up into the hay to the back wall and called to me quietly.

"In return I gave him a suppressed groan.

"Then he resolutely removed the clump of hay I had closed my entrance with to hold in the heat, and he made the opening bigger so he could come down to me.

"I turned away from him.

"I whimpered, 'Leave me alone. You can't be here.'

"'Should I get your mother?' he asked.

"I shook my head, and a new contraction tore through me.

"'I guess there's no time to get anyone anyway,' he mumbled, pushing his way into the tight space.

"'You have to leave,' I whispered.

"'No,' he answered. 'I'm going to help you. I've received plenty of calves and piglets in my days as a hired hand.'

"'But you're a man,' I moaned.

"'It doesn't matter,' he said. 'But you have to take off those long pants.'

"'No, no, no.'

"'You have to,' he demanded, and pulled them down off of me.

"'There can't be men here,' I kept on.

"'It doesn't matter since you're dead anyway,' he said firmly.

"I understood what he meant but a new contraction kept me from speaking. I was bathed in sweat despite the cold air from the opening.

"'Lay down on your back,' he said, pushing a big pile of hay under my head. 'And bend your legs.'"

Malvina put her hands up to her face so Tacit and Ælgar couldn't see her.

"I can't tell you," she moaned. "It's too awful."

Ælgar and Tacit glanced at one another. They remembered all too clearly how it was when Mina was born.

Ælgar pulled on his beard.

"But didn't it go alright?" said Tacit. "It must have been

better with a man there than with no one at all."

"You went to get Granny," she said, lifting her face.

"We weren't as brave," he said.

"He told me that he had helped my mother one of the first times. The midwife didn't get there before the baby was born." Malvina's voice calmed down. "She had told him what to do. I don't know if was true or if he just said that to reassure me, but it helped. I held my knees like he told me and he said I should yell instead of holding it in. I could hear him as if he were far, far away. It was like I had sunk into a deep darkness and I thought that I had sunk into the peat pit after all.

"But then a new sound bored its way through to me. A wail that wasn't my own. It was the baby crying. My baby. And I struggled to come up out of the darkness, up to the surface. Magpie said something to me, but I couldn't grasp what it was. Then I felt a warm, damp weight being placed on my chest, and I put my hands up to it. It was cloth. A round, warm clump with something around it.

"'It's a girl,' said Magpie.

"When I opened my eyes I saw the knife. He sat there cutting into a pillowcase.

"'What are you doing?' I asked anxiously.

"'I'm cutting it open. I need some thread to tie off the belly button.' He said it as if he done it lots of times. I looked at Mistress's fine pillowcase with the embroidered signature.

"'Besides,' he said, 'you need two diapers more than you need one pillowcase.'

"I could see him clearly now, as he sat there pulling thread out of the cut edge.

"'Is she—is she –,' I didn't know what I was supposed to ask.

"'She is fully developed,' he answered, 'but she's not very big. She is just like she's supposed to be.'

"Relief washed over me and I sank back exhausted, while Magpie turned over the little bundle, tied the belly button and cut off the cord leaving a good bit extra. Then he swaddled the piece of cloth around the baby again and laid her next to me.

"While I dozed I could tell that he was rummaging around and scraping a bunch of hay together where the baby had been born. But it wasn't until he said that he had to go outside with the refuse that I realized what he had been doing. I gave a little cough from the depths of my torpor.

"When he came back in a bit later, with a puff of cold air around him, he asked, 'What's her name?'

"'I don't know,' I answered. I didn't want to tell him that for a long time I'd been calling her Comfort. And I hadn't at all thought about a baptismal name.

"He sat there waiting.

"Then he said, 'I could have her baptized for you.'

"Just the thought of it seemed meaningless and strange.

"'Someone like her can't be baptized,' I said. 'She doesn't even exist. She has no father and her mother drowned before she was born. She is outside the world of people.'

"'But what if she dies?'

"'Then I'll bury her. The priest won't bury people like her and me.'

"'How can you say things like that?' Magpie sounded mortified. 'Everyone has to be baptized so they can enter heaven.'

"'The priest is a person. Do you think he would bless a bastard of a bastard?'

"'But he has to.'

"'Do you think a single person in this village would bless my child?'

"That quieted him. We both knew that not even my mother would be happy about the little one.

"Then I asked, 'Do you believe God would leave it up to what people will or won't do? If there really is a God, do you think he would put the blame for what Master did to me on a little baby?

Then he's no better than people.'

"We looked at one another.

"'You have changed,' said Magpie. 'You're not at all like the girl who lived with us until the spring.'

"'No,' I said. 'She drowned. She couldn't bear living the life of a person.'

"He sat there thinking.

"Then he said, 'I think I know what you mean. I'm probably the only one in the whole village who could understand it.'

"'Because you're an outsider too?'

"'Yes,' he said. 'That's probably why.'

"We became quiet, and I was nearly falling asleep.

"'Are you doing okay now?' he asked softly.

"'Yes,' I mumbled.

"'Then I'm going to leave.' He turned to go up through my tunnel.

"'Thank you for coming and helping me,' I said behind him.

"He mumbled something and spread some hay over the entrance. I think I was already asleep before he reached the door.

"When I woke I was awash in milk. My shift and woolen underwear were soaked around my breasts, and I put the baby there immediately. The world outside was far away, like it had been before Magpie found me, but I wasn't alone anymore. The fox in the meadow barn had had a baby."

Malvina stopped talking. She sat for a long while staring into space, as if she weren't aware of where she was.

"Foxes are good animals," said Ælgar softly.

"What do you mean by that?" asked Malvina, suddenly alert.

"They make several exits," said the old man.

She didn't answer.

Tacit thought about the fox holes at Eagle Hill and nodded in agreement. "I'd better go home now," he said.

"It's starting to get light out," said Malvina. She looked

exhausted.

Still everyone stayed sitting, captivated by what she had told.

Ælgar got up first. "I'll take both children over with me," he said, repeating his offer.

"That's not necessary," said Malvina. "It'll be fine."

"It'll be better for you to sleep undisturbed," he answered gently. Ælgar picked up Comfort and nodded to Tacit to carry Mina. Malvina quickly gathered up the girls' clothes for them to take too.

The Water Farm

All the way back to Granny's house Tacit thought about what Malvina had told them. It was different and much more complicated than he had expected. He was so lost in thought that he forgot to be quiet when he went through the kitchen, and Granny emerged with her thin braid hanging loosely down her back and her bare feet in slippers, to see if there was something wrong, since he was making so much commotion.

"Why are you making so much noise, boy? Where have you been?"

"Nowhere."

"That's what you always say."

"You don't need to know everything."

"Have you been to the inn?" She tested to see if he smelled like beer.

Tacit laughed. "Not on your life. Go back to sleep."

"You go in and sleep. You have to get up soon for work."

Tacit did as she said, and in the following days he did his work meticulously while he waited for a message to arrive from teacher Melin. But when the teacher finally was able to track down the owner of the Water Farm, it turned out that he was not particularly interested in selling, and the price he named was much too high.

Teacher Melin shook his head.

In an impatient tone, Tacit asked "Why in the world would he want to keep it?"

"I don't understand it either," said Melin. "But you can't pay that much for it. You might as well let the old man keep living there like he's been doing."

"Did you tell him that someone was living there?" asked Tacit, suddenly worried.

"Of course not. I wrote to him that the farm was sadly neglected and dilapidated."

"How would you know?"

"From what you've told me. That the buildings weren't suitable for people to live in, let alone livestock, and there wasn't any land except the hole where the house was situated." Melin looked at Tacit somewhat reproachfully. "It's not worth buying," he said.

"Yes it is," protested Tacit. "I can save up for it."

"Sure, for years. And then after that it will still cost a fortune to fix it up so it's livable. You risk having insurmountable debt for the rest of your life."

"How so?" asked Tacit, not really understanding.

"Interest—interest—," answered the teacher. "They accumulate faster than you can earn enough to pay them back. And once you sign something, you're stuck." It sounded almost like a threat.

"But—"

"Get it out of your head," said Melin, taking a piece of paper and a pencil. He started calculating what the real cost for Tacit would be. Year after year after year.

"Look here. This is just the down payment. And you don't have that do you? And if you borrow it from the bank you'll have to pay interest."

Tacit stood as if paralyzed by the various numbers. How could Melin know it would be that much?

"And the bank will want collateral for its money," continued the teacher. "What do you have for security? Granny's house? As soon as you don't pay your interest on time, they'll take the house and send Granny to the parish."

"You don't know that for a fact," said Tacit in feeble opposition.

"Yes, that is a fact," maintained Melin. "That's what happens. Do not sign anything unless you can pay it. What are you? A blacksmith apprentice? And when you get your certificate there's still no guarantee that you can keep your job long enough to pay it all off—and then what?"

Tacit sat quietly a moment. Then he said, "What about that finder's fee?"

"That will only be a drop in the bucket."

Tacit sat there at a loss about what he should do. Then he asked again, "Why would they want so much money for that farm when it can't be used for anything?"

"They don't want to sell it." said Melin. "It doesn't cost them anything to leave it there. And then it's theirs if something should come up someday."

"What in the world could come up?"

"Well how would I know what they're thinking? Maybe that someone with money would want to build a beach hotel?—you know beaches are getting to be fashionable."

"Here?" asked Tacit, surprised.

"Sure, why not? It's pretty close to the water as far as I gather. And beaches are really catching on from what I hear."

Tacit sat there as if he had turned to stone. Then he said, "But they can't do that."

"Oh yes they can. Money decides what happens. They don't care about people. You know, money wants money."

Teacher Melin couldn't help but see how disheartened it made Tacit, but what mattered to him was preventing the lad from getting into something he wouldn't be able to get out of again.

After a little bit, Melin asked in a gentler tone, "Why do you want to buy that place anyway?"

"I've told you already. I like it there. And someone is living there who has no place else to go."

"Then why don't you rent it?"

"Rent?"

The word was tossed to Tacit, who grabbed it unprepared.

Rent? He sat with it as if it were a living creature.

"Sure," continued Teacher Melin. "Then it would be legal to live there and do what you're doing, as long as you pay your rent and as long as they don't give you notice."

Tacit just stared at him while he tried to think through the suggestion. Then Ælgar could live there legally—but he could also be told to leave. It wouldn't be permanent—but it wasn't as if it were now, either. Tacit didn't know what to say.

"And at the same time you can save up your money," Melin coaxed him. "You can start by putting your finder's fee in the bank—when you get it—and whatever else you can spare. They'll earn interest. And if you really are able to put together the money, it wouldn't surprise me if you could get the Water Farm for a lower price than they're asking now."

Something stirred in Tacit, an understanding he had gotten from witnessing a transaction between two important people at the market, who had had ready money.

He looked a bit uncertain at his old teacher. The thought was so new that he needed some time to get used to it.

"I'm not really sure—" he began.

"I can help you make the agreement," offered Melin quickly.

"But that doesn't make the farm mine," sighed Tacit.

"Not at first," agreed Melin.

"I'd like to do something with it, so it could be lived in," continued Tacit. "But if I could be given notice just like that—."

He thought about it. Then he asked, "What do you think they would want for rent?"

"We could find that out. I don't think it would be all that much."

"I'd like to know," said Tacit.

As he walked home to Granny's he thought about his figurines. How much could he earn with them—and for how long? That was the only thing he had in his back pocket. He could predict what his regular blacksmith earnings would be, more or less. It was the little figurines that could help him make the leap. If only he could figure out the right way to produce them.

One evening while he sat in the workshop cutting an apostle out of wax to have some models ready, the blacksmith came in and set a wooden box full of sand on the filing bench in front of him.

"What's that?" asked Tacit.

"Sand," said the blacksmith.

Tacit stood up interested. "That kind of sand?" he asked.

The blacksmith nodded, and Tacit felt the sand. It was dark grey, almost greenish. Then he took the figurine he was working on and pressed it halfway down into the grey mass and took it out again.

The impression was clear and detailed, and Tacit was happy to see how distinctly the shape was reproduced.

"Take a look," he said to the blacksmith, who bent over the box. "It's good, isn't it?"

"You can borrow it for a while," said the blacksmith.

"Whose is it?"

"Mine, dammit."

Tacit lifted his head surprised. "Why didn't you tell me about it before?"

The blacksmith shrugged his shoulders. Tacit didn't ask again; he made an imprint of the other half of the figure.

"I could solder them together," he blurted out, surprising himself with the idea. "Make them in two halves."

The blacksmith didn't answer, but let Tacit figure it out himself, only contributing an occasional unintelligible grunt. And after a good long while Tacit realized that the man beside him had something else on his mind, that the blacksmith was standing there waiting for Tacit to get over his excitement. Tacit turned partially towards the blacksmith and looked at him with a questioning expression.

"You have to do your apprentice test piece," the blacksmith informed him.

"I do?"

It wasn't really news to Tacit, but it must be quite soon, since the blacksmith said it like that.

"Have you thought about what it should be?"

"Well—a little—."

"So?"

"I was thinking about a church gate."

"Are you crazy?" The blacksmith stared at him disconcerted. "A church gate?"

"Yeah. A double one."

"That sounds complicated. Don't you think that's over your head?"

"That's what I'd like to do," said Tacit.

"Do you realize that two master reviewers from outside the parish are going to come and judge this? And they will not be lenient." The blacksmith sounded worried.

"Not really—," said Tacit ambiguously, mostly to show that he was listening.

"One with spirals, like the one in town?" asked the blacksmith.

"No, a better one," Tacit blurted out. "One with animals and leaves and flowers."

"Where is there one like that?"

"I don't know. I've seen some pictures—."

"At Teacher Melin's I assume?"

"He has a book about different trades. There's a long section about blacksmith work from olden days."

"That's going to be too complicated," the blacksmith said. "And it will take too long. Think of something else. I have to sign you up soon."

"You can put me down for that."

"You don't know what you're doing."

"Don't you think we need a new one?"

"Tell me—did someone ask you to do this?" The blacksmith was suddenly on guard.

"Not yet. But the old wooden gate is rotting."

"Do you have any idea what a custom iron gate would come to cost? What do you think the church council will say?"

"That the old one is good enough."

"What did I say?"

"But it won't last. At some point it will have to be taken down.—And then they'll know where they can get one that fits."

"Strange kind of egomaniac," said the blacksmith, shaking his head.

"It's my test piece," protested Tacit. "– and for that matter yours, too."

"What do you mean by that?"

"You have never had an apprentice before; you said that yourself. This is the first time people will see what they could learn from you."

"I haven't taught you to make leaves and flowers."

"Everything I know I learned in this smithy," said Tacit.

The blacksmith stared at him and Tacit didn't avert his eyes from the big man's penetrating gaze. And somewhere deep inside Tacit felt that he had been given permission.

"I want to see a drawing before I sign you up," said the blacksmith.

"Okay," said Tacit. His attention returned to the box of sand, and in his imagination he already saw the molten metal pouring from the ladle and flowing over the impression of the figurine.

"Did you ever use this yourself?" he asked, meaning the casting box.

Tacit turned his head, but the blacksmith had left.

Tacit sat there, feeling the desire to create seeping from his pores. It wasn't completely dark outside. He had a lot to think about. Church gates? He would have to make a drawing very soon. Little saints? He would have to figure that out. That needed to work out too. And the Water Farm?

He got up and walked over to wash his hands in the trough. He had already washed up once, so he didn't feel too dirty. Granny wouldn't have him at the dinner table unwashed. Then he closed the smithy door and walked towards the Water Farm, even though it was late.

When he grabbed the knob of the scullery door it opened on its own—it wasn't latched—and he saw a weak ring of light around the kitchen door; so they were still up.

The kitchen door wasn't latched either. He walked in and closed it behind him. Malvina sat on the edge of the bed combing her hair to braid it for the night. She was startled when he suddenly walked in and stood there in the dark without saying anything. Her hands stopped and she stared intently at him through the flickering light of the candle on the table. There lay some sewing she had been working on.

"What's wrong?" she asked anxiously.

Her eyes were big and fearful, and Tacit was sure that her heart was beating hard and fast—almost visibly even though her hair hung down to her lap. The sight of her made him forget to answer.

"What's wrong? Why don't you say something?" she asked again, pulling her naked shoulders back behind her hair. Tacit could hear her pounding heart as a shaking in her voice.

"Why don't you latch the door?" he asked, without advancing into the light.

"It doesn't latch," she whispered softly.

He reached back and shook the hasp. "Sure it can."

"There's no eye," she said in her defense.

"Why didn't you say something? You could have asked me for one."

"I never thought about it. I'm not used to latching myself in.

I've never had a door that locked." Her voice trailed off at the end.

"No," he said.

And she knew that he was thinking of the baby and everything she had told them about. It couldn't be helped. It was out now.

Nothing was spoken for a little while. Tacit saw how she sat tensely, and didn't know how to approach her without scaring her to death. What should he say? A great tenderness was just about bursting in his chest. He felt sorry for her, for everything she had been through. He wanted to be there for her, touch her very gently and carefully, her hair –

Malvina was watching him.

Why did he just keep standing there by the door? He was acting strangely, she thought. Why did he come? And so late? What did he want? That?

"Will you marry me?"

By the door, standing in the dark, he asked her without coming any closer.

The words hit Malvina and went right in. What did he say? Marry? Marry how? What did he mean by that? What did he want? She thought about Master and Tacit could see it, how she shrunk down, making herself smaller, trying to hide. So defenseless. It made him want to bang his head against the wall when he saw that. How would he ever reach her—not just across the floor, but all the way to her?

"What are you talking about?" she asked, trying to keep her voice steady.

"You heard what I said." His eyes didn't leave her. He had to get his message through—get her to understand.

"I asked if you would marry me."

"Marry? Marry how? What do you mean by that?"

"Exactly what I'm saying."

She hesitated. Her gaze wandered uneasily around the room

for a way out. She was completely at a loss.

"Can't you just say what you want? That other nonsense is too strange."

"But I did say it. I want to marry you."

She screamed. "That's just an excuse!" she yelled at him. "Don't you think I know that you're just saying that because you want to sleep with me tonight!" Her voice cracked from anger and confusion. "Don't you think I know that you think I'm someone you can just go to bed with—because I have that baby. I should never have told you about it."

She started to cry. She lay down on the bed with all her bitterness.

"That's not why I came," said Tacit from the door.

Malvina just kept crying.

"You know that's not why," he repeated, and turned to leave.

Malvina heard his clogs go out the scullery and onto the farmyard. She jumped up and ran out.

"Tacit?"

He stopped at the sloping path.

"Yeah?"

"Come here."

She stood by the corner of the house waiting while he walked slowly back to her. Her hair hung loosely, moving in the night breeze. She held her arms close to her sides as if she were cold.

"Come inside for a little bit," she asked.

He lifted his hand to touch her hair but let it fall again. He didn't dare. He would have to talk about something else.

"I'm sorry I made you cry," he said from behind her as they passed through the scullery. "I didn't mean to upset you."

"I'm sorry I reacted so strongly," she muttered and sat back down on the bed. Tacit sat at the table.

Then she asked, "Will you tell me what's wrong? Something is bothering you." Malvina looked at him soberly.

"Melin says that I can't afford the Water Farm," he answered.

Malvina studied his face, trying to read past his expression.

"Does that matter so much?" she asked quietly and carefully. She wanted to smooth things over after having yelled at him, but she also wanted to find out what really was going on.

"Maybe I can rent it. Melin thought I'd be able to."

"Why would you want to do that? Aren't things okay the way they are?" Out of habit, her fingers began dividing her hair on the one side and started braiding it.

Tacit paused.

Then he said, "I'm afraid of what will happen if it gets out that someone is living here. You have no right to live here— that kind of thing always upsets someone if they get wind of it. If I could rent the farm it would be legal."

"And what if you can't?"

They looked at one another, a long stare. Malvina searched his expression and found an unrest, an anxiety, that she had never noticed before.

"You can't leave," he mumbled. "You can't leave—."

"You know I have an agreement. I'm Granny's servant girl."

"Only for the summer," said Tacit. "And that's half gone. And that might not even matter if they discover you." His voice was different than she was used to.

"What do you mean by that?" Malvina felt like she was touching a wound.

"You can't leave," he said. "Don't disappear like the way you came."

Malvina never thought there was anything unusual about the way she had arrived. She just came. How should she answer? She braided her hair on the other side while she thought.

"Well, what I was thinking was that, if I—if we—if I had a promise—," he said hesitatingly, when she was still silent.

Malvina was puzzled. A promise? Was is really true that he wanted to marry her? How could he? After all she had told him? And when she was only fifteen?

She said it to him.

"Plus I have a baby," she added. "My mother always said that a girl with an illegitimate child could never marry a decent man. You could marry anyone."

"Yes, but you are the one I want. Why don't you understand what I'm saying?"

"Because it's so strange. What do you think Granny would say?" Malvina didn't dare put too much stock in his words.

"What do you mean Granny? Why do you think she would go through so much trouble to come out here and teach you all those things? And Ælgar—he isn't nearly as cross as before you were here."

"I've never had it as good as I have since I've lived here," Malvina admitted quietly.

"Then you say yes?"

Tacit held his breath and Malvina looked at him confused.

"To what?"

"Oh my God, you are so slow—."

She recoiled as from the flick of a whip. Tacit regretted his tone of voice and with two long strides he was in front of her. Malvina's eyes flared up in defense, and he stopped without touching her. His arms fell feebly to his sides.

"How can I tell you I care for you so you will understand that I truly mean it?" he asked sadly.

"I don't know," she whispered.

"I would never hurt you."

"No—I know—it's just—."

He waited, but she didn't say any more.

"If I come back tomorrow evening," he asked, sitting back on the chair, "will you go for a walk with me through the woods? I'd like to show you the beach."

"It's been a long time since you promised to show me that beach. But what about the little ones?"

"We'll take them with us."

Malvina looked happy.

"Yes, then?"

"I'd really like that."

Quietly he got up and said goodnight.

Hired for the Winter

Since it was late by the time he got home to Granny's, Tacit walked softly so he wouldn't wake her. His thoughts were racing, alternating between fear and expectation. First he was afraid that Malvina would leave the Water Farm that same night, that her promise about going to the beach was just a ruse for buying time. Then he thought that since she seemed so relaxed and happy in the end, she really did believe him.

Tacit regretted he had come on so strong with her. He knew she needed time, a long time, years maybe, to get over what she had been through. But that didn't matter—he could wait. Just as long as she didn't take to the road again. How would he ever find her if she left the Water Farm? He cursed himself for having frightened her. He lay turning in bed, unable to find a way to make sure he could keep her nearby until she had gotten over what had happened to her.

Outside the sun started to come up.

Tacit got out of bed, walked into Granny's bedroom, and carefully took hold of the old woman's shoulder. She woke with a start.

"What is it?"

"Nothing to be afraid of," he said reassuringly.

"Why are you waking me?"

"You have to get up."

"Is there a fire?"

"No, nothing's on fire."

"Why do I have to get up? It's still nighttime."

"I can't sleep."

"So you think I shouldn't either?" Granny started sounding irritated. How ridiculous to pull her out of bed because he's the one who can't sleep.

"You have to go out to the Water Farm," said Tacit.

"You don't mean now? In the middle of the night?"

"I'll go with you before I go to work."

"What happened?" Her irritation transformed to worry and confusion.

"Nothing yet—I don't think. You just have to be over there."

"But why?"

"I'm afraid Malvina is going to leave."

"Were you over there tonight—and overstepped your boundaries?" The old woman's face suddenly resembled an eagle's. Her head turned sharply so her beak pointed unmistakably right at him, and her eyes looked condemning.

Tacit looked to the side.

"She misunderstood me."

"Is that so?" Granny's voice was high and sharp, and now she was standing. "What happened?"

Tacit told her just how it had been.

"Didn't you tell me recently she talked about how she had been sexually assaulted?" asked Granny.

"Yes," said Tacit.

"So couldn't you leave the girl in peace?"

"But I only asked her if she would marry me."

"While she was sitting there alone, half-dressed on the edge of her bed in the middle of the night?" Granny grabbed her skirt from the chair with an impatient swipe and attached it around herself. Tacit got a clearer sense of how compromised Malvina must have felt.

"It was just that I was afraid of what would happen if one day a stranger came out there. What would she do? I thought that she wouldn't leave if she knew that I wanted to marry her."

"Well I have hired her for the summer months," said Granny.

"She told me."

Tacit watched distractedly as his grandmother got dressed and did her hair into a tight bun in the back. Now she was completely awake.

"I'll go over and get the horse while you make some coffee for us," he said when she was done.

"They're not awake yet over there."

"I'll leave my hat hanging on the harness hook so they can see who has been there," said Tacit, meaning the brimless bowl of a felt hat that he used at work.

Granny went out to the kitchen, started working to light the stove, and didn't answer.

Tacit disappeared out through the scullery, and when he returned with the horse a while later and tied it outside Granny's house, the coffee pot was already simmering quietly on the hot stovetop.

"Melin doesn't think I have enough money to buy the farm," he said, scooting his chair forward to his place at the table.

"That's something at least," sighed Granny. "That old piece of garbage isn't worth giving money for. You might as well save up for a decent house."

"I don't think Ælgar would want to live in what you call a decent house," said Tacit.

"I was thinking about you and Malvina," said Granny.

"I don't know if she would either. There's something special about the Water Farm."

"Yes, it would take a special person to want to live in a place like that. She hasn't said anything about that to me." Granny walked out to the pantry and came back with a couple of slices of rye bread and the lard crock.

"I think there's quite a bit she hasn't told you," said Tacit.

"I thought that was quite a lot when she told me how she had come to have that baby."

"Did she also tell you that she threw herself in the bog when they found out she was pregnant?"

"Oh my Lord!" Granny put her hand on the countertop to steady herself.

"Or that she lived in a barn in a meadow for six months and only ate uncooked food?"

"That poor child. No wonder she looked so spindly when she arrived here. Then she gave birth alone?"

"No," said Tacit. "Her stepfather was with her."

"A man?" Granny balked at the idea.

"It's better than no one at all," said Tacit, taking a bite of his bread with lard.

"But that he could do it," said Granny.

"I think she said something about him being used to helping on the farms—with calvings and things like that."

"A woman is not an animal." Granny poured coffee into his cup and slid it across to him.

"Anyway you can't get married just like that," she said.

"Why not?" Tacit stopped chewing and stared at her across the table.

"Because she's only fifteen years old."

"Why does that matter?"

"She needs permission from her parents."

"But she's old enough to have a baby…."

"There's a law about things like that. You need a court order."

"A law? How about a master that forces himself on her at night and rapes her? What law covers that? He could just get her pregnant and then kick her out of his house. And then when someone wants to marry her so her baby could have a father, she's not allowed to because she's too young?" Tacit was indignant.

"I can't do anything about it," said Granny. "Are you done?"

"Yes."

Not long afterwards, Tacit lifted Granny onto the horse and led them through the early morning air outside the town. The sky was nearly clear, with just a few high clouds. Granny sat looking around satisfied. It had been a long time since she had been out on such a ride at that time of the day.

When they reached the road by the Water Farm, Tacit held the horse and was about to lift Granny down.

"But aren't you coming too?" she said.

"No, not today."

"Don't you want to know if she's there?"

"Actually, I do. If there's something wrong, come right out again so I can see you. Then I'll come down," said Tacit.

"So you don't want to talk to Malvina?"

"Not before tonight. You're the one who has to talk to her today."

Granny looked at Tacit with a hopeless expression and let him lift her down. Then, shaking her head, she started down along the path. Why was there always something going on with that boy? Where would it end? Why couldn't he just have a job like everyone else and let things alone? Like Mikkel had done. Sometimes she thought about what Mikkel would have said to all the crazy ideas that boy got. But maybe Mikkel would have just been proud of him—he never had a son.

Should she be proud of him, too? And all his schemes? Usually she was just afraid that he would get into trouble somehow. But now he was pretty much grown up—really—did he say married? Nineteen years old? Well, it was his life—the girl was alright—regardless of how badly she's been treated. Just as long as he doesn't go and get her pregnant again right away. Poor girl, she's barely made it past her own childhood.

Granny looked back towards Tacit as he stood there waiting next to the horse. Then she turned past the corner of the house and stepped into the scullery.

Malvina awoke at the sound of steps in the house and sat up. She could tell it wasn't Ælgar. His footsteps sounded different and he never came so early.

When she saw it was Granny coming through the door, her anxiety changed direction. Was she here at this hour because something was wrong with Tacit? Did something happen to him? Had he changed his mind about wanting to marry her?

Granny could tell there was something worrying Malvina. She said good morning and excused herself for coming so early.

"I just had to be sent out here as soon as possible," she said.

Malvina didn't look away from the old woman.

"Why was that?" she whispered.

"I guess it was mostly to make sure you didn't leave today."

Malvina smiled weakly.

"I haven't thought about leaving," she said quietly.

"I would be very disappointed if you did," said Granny gravely.

"We have an agreement that I work here."

"And I would also like to hire you for the winter, if you can stand living here."

"I've never had it so good in my whole life," said Malvina. Granny could tell that she meant it. "I would like to stay. Have a seat and I'll make some coffee."

Malvina got out of bed without waking the two children.

Granny said that she already had her coffee. She noticed, with satisfaction, that the ash had been removed from the stove and new kindling placed inside so it was ready to light.

Malvina returned to the bed and got dressed quickly. She did her hair, with braids in a circle around her head.

"Is Tacit coming in?" she asked.

"He rode back. He was afraid to come in. He's not like other people. He always does things his own way."

"He almost scared me to death last night when he came barging in. He yelled at me because I hadn't locked the door."

"You didn't lock it today, either."

"There's no catch. It doesn't lock."

"He said you threw him out."

"He left because I thought he had come just to go to bed with me. I was furious."

"He said that he proposed to you."

"Proposed?"

"Yes."

"But we aren't even boyfriend and girlfriend. And then he's standing there in the dark by the door asking if I'll marry him. So I figured…."

"He was really upset. He didn't sleep last night. He came and woke me up at sunrise."

"But he'll come by later, won't he?" asked Malvina. "He promised to take me down to the beach." Malvina's voice went soft when she spoke and she blushed a bit, which Granny couldn't help but notice.

Over in the bed, Mina awoke and sat up. When she saw the old woman sitting there she crawled right across Comfort to get down quickly.

After she had gotten a hug, Granny asked her, "Couldn't you have crawled around Comfort?"

"Why?" said Mina.

"Because it hurt her and now she's crying."

Perplexed, Mina looked away from the old woman to the crying baby in the bed.

"Don't you think you should go over and say you're sorry?" said Granny.

Granny stood up, took Mina's hand and walked to the bed. "What do you think we should do to make her happy again?"

"Pick her up," said Mina.

Granny picked up the little one and the baby stopped crying to stare at the old woman.

"Next time you can crawl around her, right?" asked Granny. Mina nodded, relieved.

"And now you'd better get dressed," said Malvina. "Then you can go call Grandpa to have his coffee."

"And bread and jam," said Mina excitedly. "Malvina made jam."

Granny smiled. It didn't take Mina long to get ready.

Mina came jogging back. "He's not there," she said. "His bed's empty."

"Maybe he's outside," said Granny.

"No. Yellow Ingelin is gone too."

"That's too bad," said Malvina. "We'll just have coffee without him. Granny has been awake for a long time already."

They sat at the table.

"He's fishing a lot these days," said Malvina. "He cuts them up and hangs them to dry. He says it's for the winter."

"Ælgar must be figuring that you'll be here for the winter, too," said Granny.

"I guess so," said Malvina.

They ate breakfast. Mina sat holding a large piece of bread in both hands with jam smeared on both her cheeks.

"You don't think we could just send someone out to talk with your parents and get a signature?" asked Granny.

"Oh no," said Malvina with a guarded expression.

"Wouldn't your mother be glad to know that you are doing alright?"

"But I'm dead...."

"To the village you are, but do you have to be to your mother, too?"

Malvina hesitated.

"Think about how you would feel if Comfort were taken away?" said Granny.

Malvina's knuckles went white.

In an aggressive tone, she asked, "What kind of signature would it be?"

"You know that you two can't just go and get married...."

"Who says we're going to get married?" yelled Malvina.

"No one yet. But if you do some day, it would be good to know."

"Know what?"

"That you can't go and get married when you're so young. You would need a court order and that requires parents' approval."

Malvina just looked at her.

Granny paused. Then she said, "Maybe Tacit could go alone. No one knows him where you're from."

"How long before we're not too young?"

"For you it will be a few years yet."

"I don't want to get married," said Malvina.

"Maybe not, but now you know, in case you want to some day."

After a long pause, Malvina said, "If my mother gets visited by a strange man, people will find out that I'm not dead after all. What would she say when people ask?"

"Did people ever find out who got her pregnant way back then?"

Malvina shook her head and looked away.

During the course of the day, Granny returned to the subject of Malvina's future, and once in a while she mentioned Tacit— what he was like as a boy, how headstrong he was later on, and all the mischief he got into.

Malvina smiled to herself, and Granny kept an eye on Malvina's expression.

In the afternoon, Ælgar returned with a string of fish hanging over the horse. He was surprised to find Granny at the farm on a regular day.

"Is there something wrong?" he asked.

"No, nothing's wrong," Granny answered with conviction. "Tacit thought it would be good for me to spend the day out here."

Ælgar looked at her suspiciously, as if she were hiding something. But the mood in the kitchen was light and he quickly settled down to cleaning the fish.

"Is the boy coming back to get you after work?" he asked.

"I guess so," said Granny.

"Since you're not home to make dinner you can both eat

here."

"That sounds good," answered Granny.

"My mother could make some damn good fishcakes out of one like this," he continued, holding up a rather large cod by its tail.

"I bet Malvina could do that too," said Granny.

Ælgar looked out playfully from under his bushy eyebrows.

"That sounds good," he said.

Malvina stared terrified from the one to the other and Granny laid her hand comfortingly over Malvina's.

When he was finished with cleaning the fish, Ælgar laid the large cod in the scullery and left with the rest.

"Where is he going with them?" asked Granny.

"He hangs them up in a row over in the gateway," said Malvina, glancing anxiously at the large fish he left behind. "I don't know how to make fishcakes out of that," she mumbled.

"Good," said Granny. "Here is your chance. Do you have any eggs?"

"Yes."

"And you have milk. What about salt, pepper and flour?"

Malvina nodded.

"And fat to fry it in?"

Malvina looked in the lard crock and said yes.

"And a knife to chop with?"

Malvina hesitated. "I don't think so. I haven't seen one, anyway."

"Then we'll have to use the bread knife. Parsley?"

Malvina shook her head.

"Not even self-seeded ones?" Granny gave her a questioning look.

"I don't know."

"We'll go out and see," said Granny. "There must have been a garden here once, even if it was a long time ago."

Granny took Mina by the hand and Malvina picked up

Comfort and they walked around the different farm buildings for a look time, looking for somewhere where there could have been a garden. But everywhere the ground was terribly uneven.

Granny mumbled irritatedly to herself. "Why would he want such a miserable place? There's not even a spot where parsley could survive."

"Next year I'll put some in the potato bed," said Malvina.

"Have you set any onions?"

"Only a few. I put in the smallest of the shallots you gave us."

"Smart," answered Granny. "Can I see them?"

They walked over to the potato patch and Malvina showed her the onions.

"There's not much of a root yet," said Malvina.

"Maybe not, but there's a good top on them."

Malvina looked puzzled at the old woman.

"Top?"

"Instead of parsley sauce we'll make it from onion greens." Granny bent down, cut a single onion green from each set and brought them inside.Then she showed Malvina how to cut fillets from the cod and remove all the bones. Then she set the girl to chopping one piece of fish at a time on the cutting board before putting it in the baking dish. Meanwhile, Granny lit the stove and put the skeleton in the smallest pot she could find.

Malvina glanced at her but didn't ask her anything. In the middle of their preparations Tacit came riding down the wheel-track, across the farmyard and over to the water trough where he got down and let the horse drink.

"I guess he couldn't wait for the end of the day," mumbled Granny to herself when she saw him.

Malvina turned her body a bit so she had her back to the door.

"You're early," said the old woman, when he came inside.

"I promised Malvina to take her to the beach this afternoon," said Tacit.

"She doesn't really have time right now," said Granny.

Tacit walked over to see what Malvina was doing. She tried to act as if he weren't there.

After he had stood there for a while, Malvina asked, "Do you happen to know if there's a chopping knife anywhere?"

"Hm," he considered. "I'm not sure. Whatever I've found I've stuck up underneath the roof eaves all around. I can go out and take a look."

He left, and it was quiet in the kitchen for a long while.

Then Malvina said, "Maybe Ælgar knows. He always hides whatever he finds."

Long after they were done with the chopping and blending of the mixture, and already were starting to fry it into fishcakes, Tacit came in with something in his hand.

"Did you mean something like this?" he asked, holding out a stump of rusty metal.

They both turned to look.

"Yes," said Granny. "But that one looks like it's too rusted to be used any more."

"Don't say that. If the blade gets sharpened and hammered out, and gets a decent wooden handle...." He looked hopefully at Malvina, who nodded her approval.

"Don't you think it's too far gone?" asked Granny.

"You can try at least," said Malvina, looking directly at Tacit.

He laid the chopping knife on the doorstep outside so he would remember to take it with him. Then he asked Granny why she was cooking the fish skeleton.

"How do you think you make a good sauce?" she asked him in return. "From flour and water?"

He backed out of the kitchen and walked over to look in on Ælgar. The two didn't return until Mina came running to get them.

After they were done eating, and Ælgar had praised the fishcakes, Granny said that she would clean up. So they could leave.

"What?" said Ælgar.

"I don't mean you. The young ones."

"What do they have to do?" He seemed confused and a bit offended, since he wasn't included.

"They're going down to the beach," said Granny, collecting the plates. "Malvina has never seen a beach."

"She hasn't? Well…." Ælgar stood up to leave with them.

"Come back here and sit down," she said. "It's enough that they're taking Mina. You can have Comfort." She picked up the baby from the bed and laid it in the arms of the old man, who sat back down on the chair.

Outside, Tacit, Malvina and Mina walked out through the gateway where Ælgar's fish were hung to dry. They looked up as they passed through.

Tvi Henfoot

The walk down to the beach was longer than Malvina had expected. They walked far, through tall woods with thick old beech trees on a path that wound up and down and back and forth. At one place on the right, a burbling stream flowed into an oblong, totally black woodland lake that was completely surrounded by large overhanging trees.

Tacit led her over there.

"This is where Nøkken lives," said Tacit gravely.

"Who?" Malvina looked around for something resembling a house or a hut, but there was nothing there. Only bushes and trees.

"Nøkken," repeated Tacit.

"Where?"

Tacit pointed into the black water.

Malvina took a step back. She remembered all too well how something had pulled on her legs when she was in the water in the peat pit.

"Who is that?"

"Once in a while he surfaces and sits on a toppled tree trunk or plays music on something old people call a felay. He's very attractive, with long hair like a woman's and a crown of lilies on his head.

Malvina stared at him with round frightened eyes.

"Did I scare you?" smiled Tacit.

"Don't joke about things like that," she said.

"It's just a story."

"He might have been the one who grabbed at me when I was in the peat pit."

"But he doesn't really exist," said Tacit, now regretting what he had told her.

"How do you know? You don't know everything."

Malvina returned to the path with little Mina hanging on her skirt.

"Why does he live down in the water?" asked the child with a worried voice.

"He doesn't live down there," answered Tacit. "He went back to where he came from."

"Where is that?" Mina looked doubtful.

"Far away. Very, very far."

"How do you know?"

"Because that's where he is. Someone saw him back in his own country."

"Oh, you are such a liar—to tell a child things like that." Malvina pulled Mina close and put her arms around her.

"You should have heard the stories Granny told me when I was little," Tacit said.

"That is no excuse," said Malvina.

They walked the last stretch of the path without even noticing it, and suddenly they were out on a grassy slope from where they could see the ocean.

Malvina stopped, thunderstruck.

"What is that?" she whispered, overwhelmed.

"That's the water," said Mina, as if it weren't anything special. "That's where Grandpa goes fishing."

The sight of it made Malvina go weak. She just stood there until Tacit took her hand and led her down through the grass. Mina skipped and ran ahead of them.

At the bottom they reached the sand, white and inviting, with an edging of stones and seaweed just past the water's reach. Malvina noticed that Tacit kept holding her hand. Then Mina waded out into the shallows where the breakers came and went.

Malvina went to grab after her.

Then she blushed a little and pulled her hand back.

"It's not dangerous," Tacit said. "It's so shallow here at the shore. You can swim in it."

Malvina didn't believe him. She kept an eye on Mina at all times until the child came back to the beach and started collecting empty seashells. Then Tacit got Malvina to sit down on the dry sand higher up.

"It sure is strange," she said.

"What is?"

"That there's no land on the other side."

"There is. You just can't see it."

"Why not?"

"It's too far away."

Malvina didn't respond. She just kept staring.

Then Tacit asked, "You didn't pass any beaches while you were making your way here back then?"

"No," said Malvina. "I was in the country. There was snow," she added.

"Wasn't it hard to walk, carrying a baby?" asked Tacit carefully.

"Yes," said Malvina without looking at him. "There was a lot of snow. I got to her house at night."

"Barefoot?" He looked at her legs.

"No," she said. "It was almost like boots. Since I couldn't fit my clogs with socks on anymore, I put my clogs on first and then pulled Mistress's long wool socks on overtop."

"The ones you took off the clothesline?" Tacit smiled.

"Yes."

"Did you go far that day?"

"The first few days I walked as far as I possibly could. I didn't stop except to rest in a barn or an outbuilding, where I could steal a field beet, gnaw off as much as possible, and carry the rest with me. Sometimes there was some cracked grain."

"Is that what you had at that old woman's house too?"

"I didn't think there would be anything there. It was just a tiny house, and I was going to go right by since there was no path. No one had walked in the snow outside. The place was set back from the road a bit, and almost hidden by bushes. I walked over just to see if there was a place where I could nurse Comfort. Neither the front door nor the barn door had been used since it snowed, but I thought I could rest inside the barn. At least we would be out of the weather.

"I walked over to the barn door. But I was still a bit afraid. What if the people who lived there were sick, or even dead, and all the animals too?

"I stood listening first, but I didn't hear anything. So carefully I opened the latch with both hands not to make any noise. Then I opened the top of the dutch door a little, and sniffed to see if it smelled like death."

"And?" said Tacit.

"It smelled like a barn. A real warm living barn with animals in it. So I stuck my arm in and found the latch to the bottom half of the door, stepped inside and shut it carefully behind me."

"That was daring," mumbled Tacit.

"I had to. You can't sit outside in the snow and nurse a newborn."

"No, but still."

"It was also very dark," added Malvina. "Outside the sky was clear with stars and a few clouds, but inside it was a different kind of dark, dense as wool and without the least bit of light anywhere, as if there weren't any windows. It was like I was blind and I felt my way with my feet and my one hand. I held Comfort tight with my other arm underneath the heavy wool blanket I had around us.

" I could tell the floor was stone, and I moved my feet slowly, and silently, because the socks were on the outside. The whole time I held out my one hand until I bumped into some wood. It felt like a partition or a pen. I ran my hand along the top edge and walked along the side. Something came over and very gingerly sniffed my fingers, inspecting me; then it pulled back again. I kept moving my feet carefully, one at a time, holding Comfort close so she wouldn't cry.

"Then my fingers bumped into a hen that was sitting on the partition. It rose up startled, cackled indignantly, and then settled back down to sleep. My fingers became sensitive as feathers. There was another hen, and another. Then the partition ended at a thick vertical post.

"'A cow pen,' I thought, and I held out my arm to find the cow—moved it back and forth—but maybe it was lying down?

"I lowered my arm and bent over a bit, feeling around where I thought it would be. And my hand grazed something. A kind of skin without fur. It felt kind of cool, and I let my fingertips move across its surface. Did it have a rash? Was it dead? I gasped and pulled my hand away.

"It was a hand—a cold human hand.

"My heart was beating so hard I thought anyone could hear it from across the barn. A hand on some clothes. So there was someone dead in this place.

"I just stood still for a while, listening. I could hear some animals around me moving, and breathing quietly as if they were sleeping. It didn't sound like sick animals. They sounded fine, but I had to restrain myself to keep from darting back out the door.

"'Who are you?' said a crisp old voice quite close to me."

Malvina paused. Tacit could tell by her breathing how terrified she had been.

"I didn't know what I should say," said Malvina. "I was too scared. And the voice asked me again. I thought it was the dead person talking to me. That the spirit was still in the barn."

Tacit almost didn't dare to breathe for fear of interrupting Malvina and breaking the spell of the story. As she was telling it, she was reliving the experience. She had forgotten she was sitting on an exciting new beach, next to water that was bigger than she had ever seen.

Malvina continued. "'I didn't think anyone was in here,' I whispered back."

"'What is your name?' asked the voice.

"'Malvina Mandsdatter,' I answered. I had already decided that—back in the meadow barn."

Tacit nodded. That didn't surprise him.

"'Where are you from?' asked the voice.

"'From the road.'

"'That's not what I mean. Where do you live?' It sounded like the voice of a very old woman who hadn't said anything for a long time—thin and hoarse.

"'Nowhere,' I said.

"'Is that so,' she said, 'as young as you sound, you must have a home someplace.'

"'I'm a wayfarer,' I said.

"'You must have parents somewhere—and a home?' She seemed so certain, that I wasn't sure how to answer.

"'Not anymore,' I said.

"Then it was quiet for so long that I thought the spirit was at rest again.

"'Then you're alone?' she asked again.

"'Yes,' I said, figuring that Comfort was part of me.

"'Then come up here in the bed,' she insisted. 'It's cold to walk around at night.'"

"The bed?" asked Tacit surprised.

"I was taken aback," said Malvina. "But then I felt along the post and noticed that there were boards nailed together in front of the cow pen, and that it was filled with straw. I could hear it rustling as she pulled it aside. She was a live woman lying there.

"'Come in here where it's warm,' she said.

"Carefully I sat down on the edge and unwrapped Comfort.

She started complaining immediately while I removed everything I had wrapped around her.

"'What do you have there?' the woman asked curiously.

"'My baby. I came inside to nurse her.'

"'Oh, you have a baby. How do you like that.'

"I crept into the bed and spread Mistress's wool blanket and my wool shawl over us. Then I loosened my clothes in the front and put Comfort to my breast. She was cold and very hungry.

"Meanwhile the old woman lay there whispering very quietly to herself, as if there were something she were trying to figure out. As if she were searching her memory for something she had forgotten. Then it was quiet for a long while and I thought she had fallen asleep. But she wasn't sleeping. As soon as I moved, she asked me when the baby had been born.

"'Three weeks past mid-winter,' I said, which was the truth.

"'And that's why you don't have any home any more?' she said.

"To that I could only answer yes.

"Then she was quiet again while Comfort drank and all I could hear was the breathing of the animals.

"'You come from down by the bog, don't you?' she asked suddenly.

"It made me jump when she said that. I thought I had traveled quite far from my village.

"'You're the one who drowned herself last summer,' she continued.

"She noticed, by my lack of response, that she had caught me off guard, and she gave a cackling laugh.

"'How did you know that?'" I asked.

"'It gets around when someone drowns herself,' she said. 'People talk, and word gets around. I've heard about you.'

"'What have you heard?'" I asked anxiously.

"'That you couldn't rest in peace because they couldn't bring you up. You didn't get a proper burial.'

"'And what else?'

"'That you went and took your burial shroud from your mistress's clothesline and that you were seen around the village at night—and still are. No one dares go out after dark. Your mistress isn't really herself anymore. And they say your master isn't doing so well, either. Bad things have been happening to them.'

"The woman stopped talking. Evidently she could tell I was thinking of leaving. I didn't have to say it. She had this special way of sensing what people were thinking. She knew who I was.

"'There's no need to be afraid,' she said. 'You don't have to leave. I'm dead, too. I die every autumn.'

"I thought to myself, 'That was why there were no tracks in the snow outside.'

"'That's right,' she said. When she breathed it made a faint whistle.

"'Every spring I'm amazed that I'm still here,' she said.

"I held my breath when she said that," whispered Malvina.

Tacit didn't dare move and disturb Malvina's story. But Malvina stopped on her own and was silent for a long while.

"But who was she really, the old woman?" asked Tacit.

"She said she called herself Tvi," said Malvina.

"Tvi? Doesn't that sound kind of like a swear?"

"I asked her about it because I thought it was a strange name," said Malvina.

"Tvi said, 'That's what they yell at me when they see me. The children yell that. Because that's what their parents say under their breath when they see me come hobbling.'

"'Why do they do that?' I asked.

"'Because they're afraid of me. Afraid I'll put a curse on their house, afraid I'll put a spell on their animals so they die in the fields. They won't let me inside their barns because they're afraid it will put blood in their milk. They won't let me inside their houses. I can only work for them if it's with things that aren't alive—gathering wood and weeding and things like that. And when I work there's always someone keeping an eye on me, so I don't draw signs in the ground or make crosses from sticks or anything like that.'

"I asked, 'But can you do those things?'

"'It's enough that they think I can,' she said.

"'It's also because I walk so poorly,' she added a bit later. "Almost everyone calls me Henfoot.'

"'Why do they do that?' I asked, hoping to lead the conversation away from the blood in the milk.

"'It's because I'm missing so many toes,' she said. 'There's so much room between the ones I have left that no one likes to look at them. But they still stare at my feet.'

"So I asked her if she was born that way, but she wasn't. She said they froze off when she was very young. It was while she was employed somewhere where she had to gather firewood in the forest, and no one paid any attention to what she had on her feet. She said that winter was very cold, and some of her toes turned black and shriveled, and they broke off one by one. She said it was a very long time ago.

"I told her I was startled when I touched her by accident, because I thought she was dead.

"'I am dead,' she answered, with emphasis.

"'I said, I'm glad I could come inside here and nurse the baby.'

"Her response was, 'This is no weather to be out in with an infant.'

"'I couldn't stay in the meadow barn any longer,' I told her. 'They would be coming to get the hay soon.'

"'You can stay here with me,' she said.

"I told her I couldn't stay. I had to get farther away.

"'You are farther away than you think,' she said. 'It's a long way back to your village.'

"'But you've heard of me,' I said. I turned my face towards her, though I couldn't see anything at all in the soft, thick darkness.

"She didn't answer.

"'I'm old,' she said instead. 'But I have a house. They said I could live here if I wanted to. They didn't want me in the village. You're young and strong. We could help each other.'

"I didn't answer and we lay down to sleep.

"Much much later I asked, 'How come it's not getting light outside?' I was worried that something had happened to my eyes, that they had turned black and shriveled up from being out in the snow and cold for so long.

"It didn't help my fear any when Tvi answered that of course it had been light out long ago.

"Alarmed, I asked. 'But can you see any light anywhere?'

"'No,' she said. 'You're not supposed to.'

"I didn't understand.

"'I make the nights longer,' said Tvi.

"I thought about what she had said about hexing the animals. Then I asked if she didn't think the nights were already long enough in the winter.

"'By extending the nights, the fodder lasts longer,' she answered. 'We sleep away as much of the day as possible.'

"She slid down to the foot of the sleeping area and found her clogs with her feet. Then she clomped off in the direction of the door, where she fumbled with something. Then suddenly daylight streamed in like a thick column through a hatch in the front wall. And then after a little bit, another one was opened. The change was overwhelming.

"Tvi placed the two hay sacks that had been stuffed into the window openings down by the wall and came back to the bed. Meanwhile all the animals in the barn started reacting. The one chicken, which revealed itself to be a rooster, still standing on the pen partition, started crowing piercingly loud. I saw that I was sitting in a rather small stable.

"In the pen opposite me a cow stood up and mooed, and a little disheveled dog that had been lying asleep on the cow's back tumbled down and started barking when it noticed there was a stranger in the room. No matter where I looked there was something moving that wanted to eat.

"A goose and gander sauntered by with their necks outstretched, hissing over the bed frame, and a number of cats appeared suddenly without my seeing where they came from. Two sheep and a goat stuck their heads over the edge of the pen next to mine. They were the ones who had breathed so gently on my fingers the night before. And from some hidden place a pig was screeching. The transformation from the blanket of peaceful darkness was paralyzing.

"Tvi's mouth was moving, but I couldn't hear her, so she laughed and started the feeding. Hay for the cow, sheep and goat; potatoes and apples that she crushed in the trough with her clogs for the pig, and the geese and chickens started to help themselves to it even while she was still stomping.

"Then she milked the cow and put a lid on the bucket so the cats wouldn't attack the milk. They got theirs from the goat, just like the pig did. Gradually the commotion started to subside, until little Comfort's heart-wrenching cries could be heard. She had never in her life heard any sounds louder than a human voice. It was a long while before she calmed down.

"Finally Tvi doled out water from a large wooden trough near the door at the back of the house. Then she opened the back door and brought in new snow that she dumped into the trough until it was completely full.

"I couldn't help her with anything. I had enough to do trying to calm down my baby. And I sat on the bed thinking that she must have slept with all her clothes on. Next to me lay a comforter that she had pushed aside, and a long pillow that had been under her head. And there where I had been lying was the big pale woolen blanket—which she had called my burial shroud—all crumpled up.

"Eventually it was quiet again, and Tvi came over to get a look at Comfort.

"'You sure do have an awful lot of animals,' I said to her.

"'I sure do,' she sighed. 'That's what happens when I'm able to keep them alive.'

"I didn't really understand what she meant. I put Comfort down to change her.

"'They give me all their runts as payment when I do work for them,' said Tvi.

"'Runts?' I asked, while I looked around and didn't think I saw anything malnourished.

"'They always have one thing or another they figure is good enough for me,' said Tvi. 'A sack of soft potatoes, a barrowful of apple drops, a calf that doesn't look like it's going to make it, a lamb that the mother ignores, a pig that's born too small and won't survive, or a barrel of grain that got wet.

'On the farms no one has time to take care of things like that. "It would all just go bad anyway," they say. So they give it to me as payment. Once I was given a big gosling that had a defect in one leg. It kept coming out of joint every time it tried to walk on it. It would never walk, but it could brood. I begged for a few fertile eggs as payment the next year.'

"'What about that one there?' I asked, wondering, pointing at the huge cow, which was standing quietly, munching down hay. 'Was that a runt once?'

"Tvi nodded.

"'I carried that one home in a sack,' she said. 'It couldn't stand up or eat. It's stomach was distended and its excrement ran out thin as water in a ditch. I didn't think it was going to make it.'

"'Well, what did you do?'

"'I stayed with it as much as possible. I became its mother. I talked to it, kept it warm, and kept trying to find something it could eat. It wouldn't take milk, and it seemed in pain if I tried to force anything down it. It felt best when it didn't eat, so it was just going to lay there quietly until it died.

'It was early spring and the grass wasn't hardly growing yet, but I got down on my knees and plucked tiny blades of grass for it one by one. I also picked the buds on the trees and put them in its mouth one at a time. And one day I came out here and it was standing up.

'So I tied a old wool vest around it so it wouldn't lose the small amount of body heat it had, and I took it outside and just walked it around. Just a short walk the first day, but more and more ever since. And every time I paid attention to what plants it ate, and I picked more, and I brought them back with us. But it wasn't until the beech hedge behind the house leafed out that things really turned for the better. It pulled off beech leaves and only beech leaves, and it got stronger and stronger from them, and now there you see it.

'And everyone says it's from witchcraft,' Tvi added bitterly."

Malvina sat quietly, staring while her fingers sifted the fine sand.

Then Mina asked suddenly, "And what then?"

Malvina and Tavs realized that Mina was sitting very close to them and not playing, with all her attention turned towards Malvina and her story. They looked at Mina and smiled.

"Why didn't she have any toes?" asked the girl, and they realized that, for a long time, she had been paying more attention to the story than playing with shells.

"Because they had fallen off," said Malvina. "A long time ago when she was a little girl there was no one looking after her when it got cold to make sure she had wool socks on."

"And then her toes just fell off?" Mina looked scared.

"That's right. You have to be careful when it gets cold," said Malvina.

"Grandpa is going to make me boots for the winter. He said so himself," said Mina.

"You are lucky to have a grandpa like that," said Malvina.

"Yes," said the girl, nodding.

"And what then?" asked Tacit, just like Mina had done.

"Nothing then. I lived with her for a while—until the spring work started on the farms and she wanted me to go work while she took care of Comfort."

"And you wouldn't?"

"I couldn't. It was still too close to the place I was from. If Tvi could figure out who I was, then other people could too."

The Garden of Eden

Tacit arrived with the measurements of the existing wooden church gates, and he wrote them on the wall of the smithy, just inside the door, where the wall wasn't quite so dark.

"But it probably needs to be taller," he said.

The blacksmith scowled. "Why?"

"Otherwise it won't fit."

"What won't fit?"

"Everything it needs."

The blacksmith grumbled to himself. He didn't like all of Tacit's ideas.

"Why can't you just make some plain bars, if it absolutely has to be a gate?"

"Bars are boring," said Tacit. "It has to be something with shapes, and things that weave in and out together."

"That's going to take a lot of iron."

"I'll make a list of materials," said Tacit. "I'll need different thicknesses."

The blacksmith pulled at his hair. He was not happy with the apprentice test project. He'd never get his money back. Why couldn't the boy just make something that people generally make for an apprentice test? Why did he have to make it so difficult? He could pass with a regular old tool that they could sell to one of the farmers afterwards. Why did it have to be so artistic? That boy's got a swollen head.

"Why aren't you making a drawing of it like I asked you to?" asked the blacksmith.

"I did that."

"Then why don't you show it to me?" The blacksmith had hoped that his demand of making a drawing would prove so overwhelming that Tacit would drop his crazy ideas.

When Tacit didn't give any further explanation, the blacksmith asked, "Well where is it?"

"Home at Granny's."

"Then go home right now and get it."

That was an order and Tacit disappeared out the door. He had hoped to wait a bit longer before showing his drawings, since almost every day he had new ideas about what to add. He returned with his hands full of pieces of paper, larger and smaller pieces of different kinds, gleaned from Granny's meager supply of letter paper, slit open bakery bags and brown packing paper.

The blacksmith was speechless. When he found his voice again, he shouted, "What in the name of God do you have there?"

"Didn't you say to go and get my drawings?" Tacit laid the papers on the filing bench.

"You can't make anything from a pile of scraps," the blacksmith categorically decided. "You might as well get that gate out of your head and make a plow with a moldboard or a harrow or something else that could be used. Throw that crap into the fire and get going. Time is wasting."

The blacksmith reached out for the pieces of paper, but Tacit quickly pulled them away.

"You could at least look at them first," he said.

"Fine, but it won't change a thing," said the blacksmith crossly.

Tacit showed him a drawing of a serrated and etched leaf with ribs and turned up points, meticulously adorned with shadows so it seemed quite lifelike.

The blacksmith twitched and straightened up. "Where did you get that," he said brusquely.

"I drew it," answered Tacit, showing him a stylized flower.

"You're crazy," said the blacksmith. "That can't be made out of iron."

"Yes it can," said Tacit, showing him a butterfly.

The blacksmith came nearer, curious. He wasn't used to looking at pictures. He was getting captivated. But then a lizard appeared with a serrated crown down its back as well as an over-sized spider with very long legs and a tiny bird with a beak like a long, curved nail. The blacksmith straightened up and gave a growl.

"Things like that don't exist," he said angrily.

"They do in some places," answered Tacit.

"How do you know?"

"From books."

"Books like that should be burned. You might as well toss the whole thing; it can't be used for anything. It can't be made, and besides, the parish council would never want to have vermin like that on a church gate."

"You don't know that."

"Well have you ever seen one?"

"There's no art in making something that other people already have made," protested Tacit. "This gate has to be unique."

"But those things are ungodly. I'm telling you I don't want that in this smithy." The blacksmith was angry now, so Tacit quickly rolled up his drawings and put them in the drawer. But that evening he took his papers and visited the priest.

Pastor Bertelsen scrutinized the young man who said he wanted to speak briefly with the priest.

"Of course, of course." The pastor stepped to the side and opened the door to his study. "We can speak privately in here," he said, in a tone that meant here Tacit could confess securely whatever was weighing on his conscience.

Tacit told him that he was the blacksmith's apprentice, and that he was almost finished, and that he had to start on his test project very soon.

The priest got Tacit to sit down while he himself went around to the other side of the table where there was a pile of papers with writing on them.

"So," he answered, waiting.

"That's why I wanted to ask you if there were any ungodly creatures in the Garden of Eden."

The priest's face took on a surprised expression, and there was a pregnant pause before he spoke.

"What do you mean?" he asked.

"I'm not thinking of the snake and Adam and Eve," said Tacit, who had an idea of what the priest would assume. "I mean all the other creatures. Weren't they, all of them, created by God?"

"Of course." The priest still seemed disoriented.

"And all of the other animals that are in the whole world are descended from the first ones that God himself created?"

The priest quickly considered the question.

"To that I would have to say yes," he said.

"Even scorpions and spiders and lizards with serrated backs from tropical countries?"

"Also trials originate from God," said the priest. "But why are you asking about this?"

"It's for my project," said Tacit. "I would like to make a wrought iron gate for the cemetery, one that depicts the Garden of Eden and has flowers and animals. But since there's not an awful lot of room on a gate like that, I thought I would only use small and overlooked animals. A frog is just as much a miracle as a lion. It's just that no one thinks about it."

"A new churchyard gate," said the priest, fascinated. "That would certainly be a needed improvement. But what is the problem?"

Tacit took his rolled-up papers from his pocket and unfolded them.

"I've made drawings of some of the animals," he said. "I've

gotten them from books about nature in other countries. But Master thinks they are ungodly vermin and he's forbidden me to make them in his smithy. He thinks they don't exist."

Tacit pushed the papers over towards the priest.

Curious, Pastor Bertelsen bent over the drawings.

"That is something," he said, after looking at them. He sounded quite impressed. "But why don't you draw on regular paper?"

"Well, I had to use whatever I could get a hold of," admitted Tacit. "What I wanted to know was if the priest thinks that things like this are ungodly."

Pastor Bertelsen's eyes scanned the spread-out papers.

"This is unusual," he said. "But it can't be ungodly to recreate real, living creatures. Could you draw for me how you imagine the gate would look?" He pushed a sheet of stationery and a pencil over towards Tacit. "Nature is diverse," he added, thoughtfully.

Tacit drew.

"These are the masonry columns," he said. "Right around here are the old hangers for the wooden gate's hinges. And then it would just be horizontal at the bottom. But at the top it would arc upwards from both sides and meet in the middle. The bars would be like plant stalks with flowers and leaves on them, and between them at the bottom there would be frogs, lizards and other little creatures. Higher up there would be winged animals, small birds, daddy longlegs, bees and butterflies."

Tacit lifted his head to discover that the priest was observing him intensely.

"That is a fabulously good idea," said the priest. "We could only dream of having such a stately churchyard gate. I will talk with the blacksmith."

Tacit felt like he was floating when he left.

Already the next day, Pastor Bertelsen appeared in all his blackness on the gravel pad outside the smithy. The blacksmith seemed disconcerted, seeing the pastor on his way to the smithy door, and he turned his questioning face towards Tacit as if he suspected it could have something to do with him. The blacksmith was secure in the fact that he and his wife faultlessly followed their church attendance, or nearly faultlessly. Once in a while he did fall asleep during the sermon. But he was in the church, which was more than one could say about Tacit.

Still he could never have imagined that Tacit would have told the priest about his plan for the wrought iron gate, and absolutely not that the boy would have presented his drawings of the Garden of Eden to him. Not to mention with the accompanying inquiries.

But the priest was barely inside the door and greeting the master before he addressed the issue. Tacit laid his hammer at the foot of the anvil, put the iron back in the forge, and started to work at something that wasn't so noisy, so nothing would hinder the priest's voice from resonating in the soot-blackened room.

"I hear that young Mortensen has to make an apprentice test project," said the priest.

The blacksmith couldn't deny that. He wondered what the priest knew about it.

"Well, he has been so considerate as to present to me his doubts as to the appearance of certain small creatures in the Garden of Eden in ancient times, which I find quite praiseworthy. And I would like to request that the blacksmith, as the young man's superior and mentor to help him understand, that at this early time there was not yet any enmity between animals and people. All were created by God and neither lizards nor insects were denied admittance to a peaceful life with one another."

The blacksmith stared dumbstruck, and more than a bit embarrassed, at the priest who had positioned himself with his back towards Tacit, thereby not needing to acknowledge his presence in the room. And Tacit felt no need whatsoever to make himself noticed or participate in the conversation. It was bad enough for the blacksmith as it was, even though the priest in no way admonished him or made it look as if Tacit had complained about him. But Tacit was sure that the blacksmith was gritting his teeth, because suddenly he was trapped and almost forced to let his apprentice make that gate. And now it couldn't be avoided that word got out about it. The priest might even mention it from the pulpit. It seemed pretty apparent that he liked the idea.

After the priest left, the blacksmith grumbled obstinately, "You sure pulled that one over pretty good."

"Who else should I have asked?" said Tacit. "The priest is the one who knows about biblical history."

"Now I have to let you make that damned gate, since you've gone and waved it under his nose."

"You would have had to let me make it anyway."

"Is that so? Who would have forced me into it?"

"Because you realize that you are the only blacksmith in the surrounding seven parishes who has an apprentice that can do something like that."

"Really. Pride comes before a fall, you know that. You're a bragger. All those books have swollen your head. Have you given one thought to how much a gate like that will cost just in iron alone? Who's going to pay for that?"

"You'll get it back again," answered Tacit casually. "That gate will be worth a lot more than the iron it's made from."

"And who do you think is going to buy it?"

"Pastor Bertelsen would like to have it at any rate."

"Of course. That's because he won't have to pay for it. The church council will—which, in the end, means the parish. And who in this parish, do you think, would give money for that kind of rubbish?"

"Then you can just sell it outside the parish," said Tacit. "They will fight over it."

"You're a fool."

The blacksmith turned on his heels and went over to his house to have lunch. Tacit covered the coals in the forge with ash and walked home to Granny's.

"On Saturday I'm going to go to town and buy paper," he said.

Granny snapped, "What do you need paper for?" in the tone she always used when he wanted to throw money away on non-necessities.

"For drawing," said Tacit.

"Nonsense," said the old woman.

"It's required when you have to make a test project," said Tacit. "Master wants it that way."

Granny didn't answer.

After lunch the blacksmith was silent. The work went as usual. No one mentioned the churchyard gate. Then the blacksmith brought it to an end when, in a rather friendly tone, he suddenly asked Tacit if he had an estimate of how much iron he would need.

Tacit fished a scrap of paper out of his drawer and gave it to the blacksmith. There were calculations for how many feet and what thicknesses.

"And you think this is enough?" The blacksmith looked doubtful. It wasn't as much as he had feared.

"I do," said Tacit. "I know we have enough scraps lying around for anything else I need."

"Then I'll ride in and get it tomorrow," said the blacksmith.

Tacit was perplexed. What happened to the grumpiness and obstinance? Was it because the priest had cleared up his fear of ungodliness? He couldn't be sure.

As soon as the blacksmith was out the door, Tacit started to root around in the scrap pile. There were a lot of small pieces there he could use, and he put them aside. In the following days he experimented. He hammered pieces flat, sawed, cut and filed edges. Flowers were the easiest, he thought, and he formed them with turned-up edges. Then he hammered the centers flat so they opened up and formed bowl-like shapes.

The animals were difficult. They had to be simplified but still create a likeness. And they had to be hammered out, yet still retain depth and precise lines. There was a lot he had to try before they were right. Just giving them an outline wasn't enough for him.

And then, there he was, with a bird or a fish that was missing an eye, or was missing a contour between a wing and the body, or was missing ribs in its fins and tail. No gills. He was going to have to invent some tools—like tiny chisels and awls, finer than anything he was used to using. And he was going to have to take some shortcuts. An eye could be a little hole with a tiny rivet through it—a round-headed nail that he nipped off and flattened on the back. He was so happy when it worked.

It was far more difficult to make figures in iron than in softer metals. But it had to work; he was determined. Tacit worked intensely, losing himself in his work, unaware of the time of day—morning and evening were both the same to him. He worked as if he were in a state of intoxication.

He had asked Granny to tell Malvina that he wouldn't be coming out to the Water Farm for a little while. But he didn't tell the old woman how actually to deliver the message. He sat in her kitchen with his drawings spread out across the table and wasn't aware of what she was saying—or if she was saying anything. And he didn't eat unless she put a plate of food right under his nose and a fork in his hand.

Then he ate. But without taking his eyes off his papers. She shook her head. It was like he was transfixed and there was nothing she could do.

The blacksmith, too, started to observe Tacit with concerned looks, which sometimes bordered on awe. The pile of failed attempts got bigger and bigger, but the number of completed figures also grew, accumulating at the back of the filing bench. The blacksmith took the liberty of looking at them only when Tacit was out making drawings at Granny's house.

Otherwise the blacksmith kept his distance from his possessed worker. He didn't get in Tacit's way. He didn't look at him; he didn't talk to him. The project was driving Tacit crazy; he was sure of that. But as long as no four-armed women with horses' legs appeared, he went along with it. The priest had approved the animals, so he yielded to that. And even though some of them looked very strange with their long serrated backs—almost like dragons—that would have to be the priest's responsibility. He himself would keep a lookout for anything obscene.

Granny stopped talking to Tacit too. He didn't hear her anyway. Instead she got her neighbor to drive her out to the Water Farm in his carriage and retrieve her the same evening. Tacit didn't notice she had been gone.

"But it will all pass eventually," she said to Malvina while she was there. "As far as I understand it, he will finish the project one day. Then blacksmiths from other parishes will come to judge what he made. I do hope he passes. But it sure is strange for a blacksmith to be sitting there drawing mice and grasshoppers." Granny sighed.

Malvina didn't answer. What could she say? She missed him. But she didn't want him to know that.

"People are talking about it," said Granny. "The priest said something about it from the pulpit. He wants an iron gate instead of the wooden one, which is old and close to falling apart."

She sighed again.

"But there will be people opposed to it," she said. "I remember when the wooden gate was going to be put in—and this is probably going to be worse."

"I hope all that work doesn't make him ill," muttered

Malvina, worried.

"He's definitely gotten thinner," said Granny. "He only eats when I make him. I hope all this doesn't make him lose his mind."

Eventually, as Tacit finished making as many animals and flowers as he thought there was room for, he switched to making leaves and stems. He still worked intensely, but now he felt the worst was behind him. And the two frames for each half of the gate didn't cause him any problems; that was just regular blacksmith work. In this way he made up for all the extra time he needed in the beginning. Now all he needed to do was attach all the numerous pieces on the frames. Even the blacksmith nodded in acknowledgement at how things were advancing.

Finally, Tacit wiped down the gates, oiled them, and burnished them black with a torch so they wouldn't rust. And very early in the morning on the day that the blacksmith judges were meant to arrive, he and the blacksmith carried the gates to the church stone boundary wall. After removing the wooden gates and setting them aside, they set each side of the new gate on its hinge posts.

They agreed it was best if the judges saw them there. Then they went back to the blacksmith's house and had their morning coffee. Tacit felt incredibly relieved, but also tired. A great heaviness descended over him. Now he could sleep.

"Lay down on the divan," said the blacksmith's wife, who could see how Tacit was drooping.

Tacit did as she said.

But in the middle of the morning, the priest came by, full of praise. He had seen the gate and he thought it was magnificent.

"Magnificent," he repeated. "A meaningful improvement." He wished Tacit good luck. Then he hurried on his way again.

A short time later the judges arrived. The blacksmith went outside with them to hear their conclusion, while Tacit lay back down to sleep. It wasn't fitting for an apprentice to hear their evaluation, only to get the final result. In the meantime, the blacksmith's wife scurried around and set the table so they could host the judges and whoever else would come to celebrate the new blacksmith.

While Tacit lay on the divan, Granny arrived and went over to him. She had been invited in light of the occasion and she was wearing her finest clothes. But she did not look happy.

She told Tacit that a lot of people were over at the church looking at the gate.

"Okay," said Tacit.

"They seem upset," said Granny.

"Upset?" Tacit wasn't fully awake yet.

"They're talking about blasphemy. About profaning a holy place. About horrible creatures where there should have been doves and crosses."

"Was Pastor Bertelsen there when you you went by?" asked Tacit

Granny shook her head.

"You probably shouldn't have made it," she said quietly.

"Of course," said Tacit. "There's nothing wrong with the gate. It's just that it probably shouldn't hang here in the village."

"What do you mean?" asked Granny, startled.

"Since they don't like it."

From outside they heard the tramping of a lot of feet, and the blacksmith's wife bent over to peer out the window.

"Oh my God. Now here they come," she whispered. "They're coming here."

And they did. Right across the gravel marched the blacksmith, his face bright red, and after him the two judges, and after them the whole crowd from the church.

Tacit got up. This was worse than he thought it would be, and he could pretty much guess on which side the evaluation fell.

The whole group stopped in front of the blacksmith's house

and the blacksmith himself ripped open the door and yelled for Tacit.

"Get out here!" He sounded like a fire-breathing dragon. Tacit had never seen him so upset, and he rushed outside.

"Well?" yelled the blacksmith, turning towards the two outsiders. "Now you can tell him yourself what you think.

It gave a start in Tacit, but they weren't going to have the satisfaction of seeing him shrink and hide. He stepped down from the entry stoop right over to them. Behind the two judges he caught a glance of several gloating faces of his old schoolmates, and behind them the condemning village residents.

The two judges hesitated.

"Out with it," said the blacksmith.

They glanced at one another.

"Not passing," said the one.

There was jeering and malicious laughter from the people behind him.

"It will serve you well, you arrogant bastard," someone yelled. "You always thought you were so high and mighty."

Tacit knew that this went all the way back to his school days, because he was quick at learning things, and because he borrowed books from teacher Melin.

Tacit looked at the judge who had spoken.

"On what grounds?" he asked.

"We don't have to give explanations," the man answered.

"Well I would have liked to know if the reason is your professional ability, your artistic knowledge or your lack of biblical understanding." said Tacit.

"You don't have to get fresh on top of everything," said the judge.

"It's not blacksmith work," said the other one.

"Then what is it?" asked Tacit.

"Some useless junk. No self-respecting church parish would hang up anything like that."

"So you didn't judge it based on craftsmanship?"

"You can easily use another year. And then present something less grandiose when you're ready."

"Let's go smash that iron piece of crap!" yelled one of Tacit's old classmates.

"No, you don't!" shouted the blacksmith. "That is my gate and you won't touch it!"

"It's blasphemous!" yelled someone else.

"We won't have it!" said a third one.

They already turned to leave, but the blacksmith stopped them.

"You will carry the gates back here," thundered the blacksmith. "Evald and Anders can take one, and Knud and Kresten can take the other one. And God help you and have mercy on you if you so much as scratch them—you will pay dearly. And make sure the others keep their fingers off."

"But what are you going to do with that rubbish?" asked an indignant farmer's wife.

"You'll find out soon enough, little Miss," answered the blacksmith. "And when you find out you'll drop dead with regret."

The farmer's wife sneered and turned her back to him.

A moment later the four farmhands arrived carrying the two halves of the gate, and they set them down inside the smithy.

"Thank you," said the blacksmith, shutting the door.

The farmhands moved back uncertainly and people started to stir.

"You can go hang your half-rotted wooden gate back up again," said the blacksmith.

The people started to disperse, and soon it was just the two judges left.

"And you. I also meant you two."

"What do you mean?" asked the one. "It is customary for us to be invited inside at these occasions."

"Do you think we have something to celebrate?" asked the blacksmith.

"But we have come from quite far away…." said the other one.

"Maybe there are some of your people there who would like to show their appreciation to you with a bit of bread," said the blacksmith, opening his hand in the direction of the retreating crowd. "But I think objectively and professionally that you should be ashamed of yourselves."

So they both turned and walked away, too.

Granny sat on a chair looking downhearted when the two came inside.

"Well that was that," said the blacksmith.

"Yeah," said Tacit, flatly.

"So you didn't become a blacksmith after all," said Granny, discouraged.

"Oh, he's a blacksmith all right," said the blacksmith. "No one can take that away from him. He just needs his certificate."

"Thank you for standing up for me," sighed Tacit.

"I should have asked for judges from the city. That's what I should have done," said the blacksmith bitterly.

"Was it really necessary to send them away?" asked his wife with a bit of reproach in her voice.

"I didn't want them inside my house," said the blacksmith.

"What about all that food?" His wife sounded irritated.

"It will all work out. It wouldn't have tasted good, eating it with them."

"So what do we do now?" asked Granny hesitantly.

"Sit down and eat," said the blacksmith. "Then we'll see."

Tacit and Malvina

While they were eating, there was a knock at the door. It was the priest. The blacksmith let him in and the new guest looked around, somewhat disoriented.

"What happened?" he asked. "Where is everyone?"

The blacksmith's wife invited the priest to the table by pulling out a seat for him. There was plenty of room; the table was set for quite a few. The priest sat down, albeit somewhat stiffly, since they expected him to. What was occupying his thoughts mostly was the sudden disappearance of the new churchyard gate.

"Where did it go?" he asked dumb-founded.

"They didn't want anything to do with it," said the blacksmith somberly.

"What do you mean?"

"The judges didn't consider it proper blacksmith craft, and our priest's own parish lambs roared about blasphemy and threatened to destroy them. So we brought them back to the smithy."

"No, no—but I had prepared them...."

The priest started to eat what the blacksmith's wife had served him, without his paying attention to what it was.

"But the half-rotten wooden gates look twice as depressing after seeing the other ones," he sighed.

"The will of the people," said the blacksmith.

"But what about Mortensen?" The priest looked sympathetically over towards Tacit. "Didn't he become a journeyman?"

"Not today," said the blacksmith.

"But those stately gates—." The priest reflected on his loss. "This is shameful, just shameful."

Tacit sat there, waiting for the blacksmith to say that he probably should have made that plow and moldboard after all. But the blacksmith didn't say that. Instead he suggested hesitantly that they sell the new gates to a church someplace else where people had eyes they could see out of.

The priest groaned at the thought. Tacit sat there, looking tired. He didn't really care any more. This last period of intense work, his excitement, and now his defeat. That it all amounted to nothing made him feel deflated. He didn't realize until now how confident he had been that he would overcome the skepticism of the rural community. Now he had his answer. He ate, but only to keep up appearances.

And Granny sat there, also sad, on his behalf. Tacit couldn't help but think about all the times he had caused her to wring her hands in despair at his crazy ideas. Evidently he hadn't grown out of that yet. He felt bad for her.

And then somewhere just outside their field of view, there was Malvina, who he couldn't bear to think about just yet.

Out on the road a carriage drove by.

Tacit didn't look up. He didn't care. Nothing mattered anymore.

"That was the parish sheriff," said the blacksmith's wife, who had gone over to peer through the geraniums.

It was a while before it made any impression on Tacit. After all, what did he care about the sheriff; he probably didn't like the gate either.

Towards the beach.

Tacit suddenly sat straight up, his blood pounding so he could hear it in his ears.

"Was there anyone with him?" he asked.

"Two women. I think the one was his wife."

Tacit looked at Granny who met his gaze. They were both thinking the same thing and they were both afraid.

"I have to go," he said hoarsely, standing up.

"Are you feeling sick, Mortensen?" the priest moved aside, dismayed.

"No," said Tacit.

"Then what is it?"

"Granny can tell you."

Tacit was out the door without saying thank you or good-bye. The door smacked behind him and all eyes were on Granny. "What was that about?"

Outside on the road Tacit tried running, but he felt dizzy and his body felt heavy and unwieldy. He was forced to walk.

But the carriage was long out of sight. He couldn't even hear it anymore. He had to try running again. Fear constricted his ribcage. And now this too, on this miserable day. He took deep breaths, steadily in and out, and that seemed to help a little. He jogged. Then he alternated between jogging and walking. Gradually he felt better and was able to speed up.

Eventually he was able to run almost normally.

Across from the Water Farm, Tacit could see the horse and carriage parked in the farmyard with the sheriff still at the reins. But he had it turned around, ready to set off quickly again. Between the carriage and the wall of the house two strange women danced around Malvina, trying to get Mina away from her. The one woman had a hold of the child's arm, while the other one pulled Malvina from behind to try to separate them. Malvina had both her arms around Mina and wouldn't let go, while she kicked as hard as she could with her bare feet and bit at them with her teeth if one of their arms got close enough.

It occurred to Tacit that she was fighting like a dog. He didn't slow down, but ran right down the wheel track. The one woman that had a hold of Mina's arm was keeping her distance, but the other woman had latched on to Malvina and was trying to pull her down.

That was when Tacit saw the knife. Malvina pulled it up from the neck of her shirt and pulled off the sheath with her teeth. Then she stabbed at the woman standing behind her.

Once. Two times. Then the woman realized it was a knife hitting her.

They both let go and started screaming, and in the wagon the sheriff rose in a flurry to help.

Malvina used the pause in the fray to put Mina behind her by the wall.

"I'll stab you if you touch me," she said. "You have no right to take her from me."

"It's a punishable offense to use a knife," the sheriff informed her, without making any effort to climb down. "You have broken the law."

"So have you!" screamed Malvina. "It is also a punishable offense to steal children!"

"I have a court order," the sheriff said authoritatively.

Malvina went pale, her eyes searching for a way to escape, when she caught sight of Tacit approaching in long, bounding strides through the grass. Without a sound she collapsed.

The two women backed towards the wagon.

"This is going to cost you plenty," gasped Tacit, trying to catch his breath.

"This is no business of yours," said the sheriff.

"You can bet it is. That's my child you're trying to kidnap."

"You're lying. I have a court order." the sheriff sat back down on the driver's seat.

"For what?"

"An abandoned child has been reported living here at the Water Farm."

"And do you think she looks abandoned?" asked Tacit, pointing at Mina.

"They said the murderer had a child living with him."

"And then you go and make a court order, drive here, and take the first child you see? If I get a court order can I come and take one of your children?"

"Of course not."

"Then what makes you think you can?"

"I'm the sheriff."

"That makes it even worse. It does your office dishonor. But I hope you can control yourself in the future. If you continue as the sheriff, that is."

"You can't threaten me. You have no witnesses."

"Look over there."

The sheriff turned his head and saw Ælgar standing at the barn gable in the driveway with a long-handled axe in his hand.

"Get up in the carriage, would you!" the sheriff hissed at the two women, who were just about falling over one another trying to climb up first.

"Make him move," the sheriff ordered Tacit, when the women were on board.

"Is your conscience bothering you?" asked Tacit. "That was the murderer's grandchild you were trying to steal."

"What a shithole," hissed the sheriff between his teeth as he got the horses moving with a yank that made the women in back grab wildly.

The carriage rattled across the farmyard and up the overgrown driveway, while Ælgar followed with the axe all the way up to the road, to make sure they really left.

Tacit went over and sat down next to Malvina, lightly stroking her hair. Her eyes were open, conscious and serious.

"If you hadn't come," she whispered, taking his hand in hers.

"Mina thought it was you and Granny," she said. "When she heard the hoofbeats she ran out to meet you, and then I heard her scream, and when I got outside they had already grabbed her. If they had gotten her up in the carriage—it's horrible to think what could have happened."

Tears streamed from Malvina's eyes and she did nothing to try and hide it.

"If they had driven away with her," she sobbed. "If they had taken her away from us.”

Tacit quietly stroked her hand and let her cry. Inside he felt happy that he was able to sit with her this way. From the other side of the farmyard Ælgar approached from the driveway. Mina, who had been distraught observing Malvina, ran over to him, seeking comfort.

“What did you do when you came out and saw what was happening?” Tacit asked her quietly.

“I’m not really sure.” Malvina shook her head and dried her eyes with the corner of her apron. “I think I just ran at them without thinking what I was doing. It happened so fast. But they were two against one, and I couldn’t hold onto Mina. Farm-women are strong.”

Tacit could tell that she was thinking of Mistress.

“I tried to kick them,” said Malvina, “but I only had bare feet, so that wasn’t enough. And that was when I took out the knife. Do you think they will put me in jail?”

“Would you have used it?”

“I did use it. But I think I only hit her clothes. There’s no blood on it, see?”

Tacit shook his head.

“You won’t go to jail,” he said.

“I went berserk. I would have stabbed them until they let her go,” she whispered. “It’s horrible to feel like that.” She tried to sit up. Tacit put his arm around her so she could lean against him. When he looked up he saw Ælgar, holding little Mina by the hand, on his way over to Yellow Ingelin. They didn’t look back. They untethered the horse and rode behind the barn through the woods.

When they were out of sight, Tacit said smiling, “Now you have to.”

“Have to what?” Malvina turned her face towards him. She was still preoccupied with the unknown carriage.

“To marry me.” Tacit gave her a tiny hug, and Malvina

became conscious of his arm around her.

"I told you I won't be forced into anything," she answered, pulling herself free from him and straightening up. "I won't marry because I have to."

"But didn't you yourself say to the sheriff that Mina was your child?"

"That's not the same thing."

"And you didn't protest when I said she was my child."

"That doesn't mean that I have to marry you. I'm not marrying out of necessity."

"Then out of what?"

Malvina looked away.

Almost inaudibly she said, "It has to be because people care about one another. It can't be like my mother."

"But I do care about you," Tacit said, almost shouting in protest.

Malvina stood up.

"How can I know that?" she said.

"Well I did ask you to marry me." Tacit stood up too.

"That's not the same. That was over a month ago."

"Wasn't Granny here? Didn't she tell you?" Tacit looked worried suddenly. Not until this moment did Malvina notice how tired he seemed. Almost to the point of exhaustion.

"Your apprentice project—that was today, wasn't it?—what are you doing here?" She put her hands up to her cheeks. "You're supposed to be at the luncheon."

Tacit took a deep inhale.

"It got scrapped," he said.

Malvina stared at him. Her eyes went dark from something happening inside her.

"But why?" she whispered. "Granny said –"

"The judges didn't like it," he said.

"Then what?"

"I didn't become a journeyman."

"But you're so talented—."

"What I made was too different." Tacit poked at a clump of moss between two stones with his toe. This wasn't at all how he had imagined he would arrive here. He had always seen himself as the victor, until now.

Then suddenly he felt Malvina's arms around his neck.

She whispered to him, "I'm so sorry it turned out like that." Her embrace was so sudden it took his breath away. But his arms unfolded on their own around her waist. He pulled her so close that she groaned. He let up a bit, but didn't let her go.

Malvina looked up at him, long and searchingly.

"Yes," she said.

"What?" he asked, wondering what she was thinking of.

"Yes," she repeated.

"Yes what?" he wanted to know.

"Didn't you just say that you asked me to marry you?"

Hesitantly, he asked, "Are you saying yes, even though I didn't become a journeyman?"

"Have you lost your hearing?"

"He bent down a little and his mouth met hers. He could tell that she had never kissed before. Her lips were hard and anxious and only gradually gave in to his. He didn't want to scare her off.

"Comfort is crying," she burst out, twisting her way out of his arms.

Tacit didn't hear anything, but he followed her into the kitchen where Comfort was crying pitifully. Malvina picked her right up and Tacit put his arms around them both.

"Wife and child," he said.

"Children," Malvina corrected him.

"I want to go back and tell Granny," he said. "I'll come back for dinner."

"And stay here tonight?" Malvina observed him soberly.

"Only if you think I should. Or for a few days," he added.

"What about your work?"

"I don't have anything now. I'm up in the air."

"It would be good for you to stay here for a little while," said Malvina. "You are almost as fatigued as I was when I came in the spring."

Tacit laughed and bored his nose into her hair. Then he left.

Granny had left by the time Tacit got to the blacksmith's. She had gone home.

"You should have seen her stop the sheriff's carriage," said the blacksmith, when Tacit was about to leave.

"Really?" said Tacit, turning toward him.

"She stood here outside on the gravel. When she heard the carriage approach, she stood still, right in the middle of the road. And she stayed standing there even though he rose up from the driver's seat shouting at her to move. She stopped his horses. She put her hands up and stopped them, even though from the look on his face he was going to run her over."

"'Where's Mina?' she asked him.

"'What are you talking about?' he said.

"'Where is the child you were after?'

"He said, 'I don't have any children here.'

"She didn't believe him and she told me to hold the horses while she searched the carriage behind the women. But she didn't find any child there.

"'Lucky for you,' she said to him.

"'Is that so?' he laughed, mocking her.

"'I would have gone to the city and turned you in,' she said.

"Then she let him drive on."

"They had a hold of the girl when I arrived," said Tacit. "Both women. Malvina had to threaten them with a knife before they let go."

The blacksmith shook his head.

"What are you going to do?" he asked.

"Marry her," answered Tacit. "Lease the Water Farm. Get

things in order. Otherwise things are too uncertain."

The blacksmith nodded.

"Should I talk with a couple of judges from the city?" asked the blacksmith. "Maybe they would give a different result."

Tacit hesitated.

"Is that legal?" he asked.

"I could always ask if a mistaken ruling can be reversed, couldn't I?"

"Thanks," said Tacit. "I'm going to move in at the Water Farm for a little while. Now I've got to go home and tell Granny."

CECIL BØDKER (b. 1927) is one of contemporary Denmark's most highly awarded and prolific female authors. She has written 59 books including poetry, novels for children and adults, short stories and plays. Her *Stories about Tacit*, a collection of 11 connected short stories, was published in 1971, forming the first book of *The Water Farm Trilogy*. Best known for her young-adult fiction books, in 1976 she received the international Hans Christian Andersen Medal for Writing for her lasting contribution to children's literature. In 1998 she was awarded the Grand Prize of the Danish Academy for her body of work as a writer.

MICHAEL FAVALA GOLDMAN (b.1966), besides being a widely-published translator of Danish literature, is a poet, jazz clarinetist, gardener, father and husband. Over 100 of Goldman's translations have appeared in dozens of literary journals such as The Harvard Review and The Columbia Journal. He teaches workshops and gives readings at universities and literary events. His recent translated books include works by Knud Sørensen, Cecil Bødker, Knud Sønderby, Marianne Koluda Hansen and Benny Andersen. www.hammerandhorn.net